FORTUNE'S DEADLY DESCENT

FORTUNE'S DEADLY DESCENT

BY

AUDREY BRAUN

The characters and events portrayed in this book are fictitious. Any similarity to real persons, living or dead, is coincidental and not intended by the author.

Printed in the United States of America.

Published by Thomas & Mercer
P.O. Box 400818
Las Vegas, NV 89140

ISBN-13: 9781935597667
ISBN-10: 1935597663

For A.R.

One may smile, and smile, and be a villain.

—Shakespeare

Once a change of direction has begun, even though it's the wrong one, it still tends to clothe itself as thoroughly in the appurtenances of rightness as if it had been a natural all along.

—F. Scott Fitzgerald

PART ONE

Benny turns five today. Waffles with summer berries and whipped cream. After that a short sail around the lake. Sometime in between will come the phone call. Benny understands, as well as can be understood at his age, that he has a birth mother named Isabel. But he has always called me Mutti and I have always referred to him as my son. Deep inside this is who he is, who we are, together. In the end Isabel got what she wanted, at least for her son. Benny will have a better life. I see to it every day.

From *A SMALL FORTUNE*

CHAPTER ONE

I close my eyes. "Tell me everything," she says. Louise Lawrence is a hypnotist with Interpol, and her goal is to make me relive the details of what happened on the train four days ago. "Whatever comes to you," she says. "Don't filter. You're safe with me, Celia." She's English, late fifties, her steely curls gathered into a bun atop her white neck. Her voice is glassy, reassuring. I try to let it lull me back to the train, to Benny and me on our way to Aix-en-Provence...but even as my rational mind knows I might retrieve some small fact that could lead us to Benny, still I resist.

"Celia…"

"Yes, I'm sorry." I close my eyes again. We're in my home office in Zurich. A CD plays trickling streams in the background, rain on leaves, birdsong, flutes. *Really?* I think at first. New Age crackpots are Interpol's secret to finding Benny? But now, strangely, I find myself letting go, being carried by her voice, and then, once more, I'm on the train.

Benny and I are in our compartment, midway between Lyon and Aix-en-Provence, when the air-conditioning malfunctions. With nowhere to go, the balmy, cagey feel reminds me of being kidnapped myself, years before, a time I don't want to think about, especially not with Benny beside me. And yet, I remember scenes so unthinkable it's as if they've been borrowed from someone else's grisly imagination.

I fasten my hair into a twist at the crown. The thin, corkscrew curls along my hairline are sticky with sweat, my legs glued to the upholstery. One by one I peel them loose, and then instinctively reach below my skirt to touch the silver-dollar-sized wrinkle in my calf, a souvenir left behind by Isabel's bullet. Yes, it's still there, and always will be, as pink and chewed as a wad of gum.

Benny and I fan ourselves with old copies of *Der Spiegel* and *Paris Match* from the magazine rack beneath the window. My fingers blacken with the ink of scandals. I consider leaving the train and hiring a driver, but we're on an express, not scheduled to stop. Besides, Benny has been looking forward to the train for so long. It's an early birthday present. He'll be eight years old in five days. I can't bear to disappoint him.

Acres of lavender whirl into a smudge past the window, and I force myself to think happier thoughts—Benny's birthday, going to Paris in a few days and meeting up with Benicio. Still, in the rising heat, I see visions of my ex-husband's Swiss Army knife—hear the sucking sound of punctured flesh, feel a burn in the white, razor-thin scars between my ribs. I remind myself that Jonathon is in a Zurich prison where he'll remain for decades. *Breathe, Celia,* I think. *Just breathe.*

"*Ich habe Hunger*," Benny says.

I glance down at his dark shiny hair, the exact color of Benicio's, his "papa," though no one would ever guess they are, biologically, uncle and nephew. I nod toward the picnic basket on the floor. "Grab whatever you like," I say.

Any minute we'll be hit with a puff of cool air. Surely. Any minute someone will know what to do.

Outside, a stone farmhouse, a scatter of goats, an abandoned, half-timbered barn mottled, oddly, with graffiti. In the distance, red-rooftop villages stack against the hills. Miles of rolling vineyards fill the space between the train and the French villagers inside their cool stone homes on a hot summer day. The light is beginning to shift. Hills become arid mountains, and a thin purple glow filters the sunlight. No wonder so many masters painted here.

A castle and its crumbling Roman wall appear in the craggy mountainside. "Look," I say. "Another one."

Benny nods.

"How is it that a country this size has castles every few miles?" I say. "Who *were* these people?" I admit I know too little of French history. Napoleon, Marie Antoinette, the gift of the Statue of Liberty.

Benny devours sliced oranges with nutmeg, then grapples with a block of homemade salted butter caramel enrobed in dark chocolate. He licks his fingers, sighs, and slumps with fatigue. I shove the compartment door open its final inch in a feeble attempt to get some relief.

Ten minutes later, it's even hotter, stuffier. Benny hasn't said a word. I glance down. "Good god," I say, and Benny laughs.

He holds his sticky brown fingers out into the shape of a tiny rib cage. Crystals of salt shine through the muck on his cheeks. "I need a napkin," he says, the whites of his upturned eyes made whiter by the chocolate underneath.

"What you need is a bath," I say. "You need hosing down." I rifle through the picnic basket...apparently in our hurry to catch the train we forgot to pack napkins.

"*Im Café*," Benny says, then switches, as he often does, to English. "I saw them next to the bottled water."

His limbs are a deep olive from swimming with his cousins in Zurichhorn Park. Strands of his hair have lightened into streaks so uniform it's as if they've been singled out and bleached. He peers up at me with an expression so much like Benicio's that I ache with longing. Benicio is in Paris doing research for a script. We've been apart for days.

I rise from my seat. "Sit tight," I say. "Don't touch anything. I'll be back in a flash." I tousle Benny's hair, it too, identical to Benicio's.

As I walk down the aisle, it occurs to me that I never indulged my older son, Oliver, now grown and living in New York City. But indulging Benny has been so easy. He's such an even-tempered, affectionate child, and what's more, he's a marvel, a kind of *food prodigy* who creates recipes with poetic names like Yellow Tuesday Chiffon and Evening Marinade. His favorite blend, *herbes de Provence* (rosemary, French thyme, tarragon, cracked fennel, and lavender), finds its way into sweet and savory alike. Last year I wrote an article for *Food and Wine* magazine about Benny's fascination with salt, his favorite Himalayan salt block, and all the recipes he's created for it—everything from peppercorn scallops to Madagascar chocolate infused with ground crystals of Haleakala Ruby salt.

It seems worth the price of sweating on this sweltering train to give Benny this adventure, this birthday gift topped off with a flight to Paris in two days and then dinner at Jardin Bleu. I can't wait to tell Benicio that the chef offered to show Benny his kitchen.

Most passengers have thrown open their compartment doors; they and their belongings are strewn about the floor and seats as if blasted by a hot, powerful wind. *Première classe* gives way to *économie*, which finally gives way to the café, a chamber of odors so thick it's like moving through a cloud of warm Brie, salty cold cuts, a locker room of perspiration. Passengers cram in line for bottled water. The refrigerated case is now empty.

As I reach for the napkins, I sense the train slowing. Pressure, a sudden gravity. I assume they must finally be fixing the air-conditioning.

I grip the counter to steady myself, thinking of Benny alone in his seat. White cattle graze in the field outside. We aren't in Aix, but it can't be far. The train shudders as it brakes, and I stumble to the side. I imagine Benny pitching forward, smearing chocolate across the seat and compartment window, down his favorite white shirt with the illustration of apple pies hanging like fruit from a tree.

"It's all right," Louise says. I realize I've gone silent and begun to cry. "Just breathe for a bit," she says.

After a moment she continues. "Tell me what you saw then, what you felt."

So I tell her about Benny's face. How everyone I've ever loved is wrapped into this child. There's Oliver's smile, inherited from Jonathon, but no matter, it's Oliver I think of when I see it. I don't like to remember that Benny is Jonathon's son too, conceived with Isabel, Benicio's sister, while Jonathon was still married to me. I like to imagine that I discovered Benny's existence in a happier way, not by hearing his cries from his crib while his mother held a gun to my head.

But there is Benicio in his face too, his dense lashes—and all his charm. It used to bother me that Benny has Jonathon's chin and cloudy green eyes, but that was years ago, when Benicio first brought him home. Now, as I steady myself at the counter, I picture Benny's little chin shifting, and I worry for him as the train slows without me there at his side.

We finally wrench to a stop in a village so remote it appears unreachable except by train. A sign reads "Saint-Corbenay" above a vacant concrete platform. Half-timbered houses line a twisty, cobbled street. The village continues down a hill, obscured from the train. I see no cars, only a red tractor alone in a vineyard. Several Dutch bikes, all black, lean against a house made of charcoal-colored stones. The depth of a Prussian blue sky is like a painting. I'm pretty sure Cézanne, van Gogh, and Picasso all once lived nearby, and I think, for a split second, that the light is so extraordinary it appears as if the sky and trees are portraits of the real thing.

One by one, the passengers in line give up, set their bottled water back in the cooler, and head toward their seats. I follow with a fistful of napkins as people cram into the aisle, chattering madly, craning to see out both sides of the train. I know very few words in French, but it's clear everyone wants to know if we should get off.

Down the aisle I rehearse what I *do* know—*pardonnez-moi, pardonnez-moi*—and am met with a dozen kinds of sneer. The heat has made us all ill tempered. It doesn't help that I can't explain my reason for pushing past. *Merci*, I add for good measure. Seven years of living in Zurich hasn't erased my American urge to smile big and long at strangers.

Warm air begins to circulate. The doors in *économie* have opened. A crowd clots in front of me. A slightly older woman seems to have fainted. Two men carry her out to the platform, while her husband and several others fan her body with newspapers and hats. They unfurl a travel-size blanket into the air like a makeshift wall to block the sun. They look Southeastern European, their eyes and cheekbones dark and wide, the women pear-shaped with dark, peppered gray hair. The way the men wave off assistance makes me think they speak even less French than I do.

Had we flown, we'd have already finished lunch, and by now be poking around the outdoor food markets. Instead, there's this miserable afternoon. Yet Benny hasn't once complained.

"*Pardonnez-moi*," I say again, without much effect.

"I'm trying to reach my *son*," I finally blurt in English. "Can you *please* move?"

Arms and legs begin to fold and turn. I retrieve my smile, my *merci* with a few *beaucoups*, and push through.

I finally reach our compartment and look inside. I check the number, look again. My purse lies next to the open *Paris Match*. Benny's backpack is gone. The picnic basket's contents are strewn on the seat opposite. There is no sign of Benny.

I dip my head into the aisle and search both ways. "*Benny?*" On tiptoes, I peer over the patchwork of heads, then crouch and squint through a thicket of legs.

I'm not yet above worrying about coming off as a fool, a hysterical American. "Benny!" I call more insistently, and then with a tinge of anger. Why would he think it's OK to wander off like this? I wipe my neck and forehead with the wad of napkins, drop them on the seat, then shove my way into the crowd. What's the word for boy? My boy. *Mon garcon*? I yell in English, "My son! Has anyone seen my son?"

The rumble of voices settles, tired faces turn toward me. "Who speaks English? Someone?" Nothing. I try, "*Hat jemand hier Deutsch sprechen?*" and the faces turn away. I thread my way to the washroom, yank open the tinny door, and am met with the stink of hot urine mixed with a sweet, flowery perfume. The faucet is running in the sink, but no one is there. Instinctively, I shut it off.

I slam the door. Panic squeezes my throat. Goosebumps flurry across my sweaty skin.

My rational mind tells me he can't have gone far. Through the window, I see that the only passengers who've gotten off are the old woman who's fainted and several others helping her. I reach the open door and lean out. The air seems scorched, fetid with manure. A string of cyclists pedal a distant road on the horizon. On the platform, the old woman has recovered and she is laughing, dazed, while her husband shakes his head.

Where is Benny?

I turn back and push my way into the next car. He must've gone this way; otherwise, he'd have passed me returning from the café.

"Has anyone seen a little boy? A lost boy?" I squeeze through more fatigued gawkers at the windows. "Please. I can't find my son!"

The train feels vast—there are only two directions to go, but there may as well be hundreds. Why did he take his *backpack*? Did he think we were getting off? He never would have picked up his beloved backpack with chocolate-covered hands. Someone else must have carried it.

A finger pecks my shoulder. I gasp and spin, expecting to see Benny's frightened eyes, but instead I'm face-to-face with a tall man whose choppy brown hair obscures half an eye. "Can I help you find him?" he asks, his accent heavy French, his teeth bright white against his deeply tanned skin. He looks like a young Picasso, round faced, the same wry stare.

"What's his name, your son?" this man asks, tossing the hair from his eye. "Give me a rundown of what he was wearing."

Rundown. The word immediately sounds wrong, as if out of an old detective movie.

I freeze. I can't remember Benny's clothes, nor can I call up the words to describe him—at that moment he's more feeling than flesh, a hole gutting me, the fleeting scent of chocolate and oranges, small arms tugging at my neck. I blink away the sweat stinging my eyes. Which shorts does he have on? Which shoes? Oh god. Something. *Anything.*

"Chocolate," I say, my eyes welling with tears. "He has chocolate all over his face and hands." A dark realization unfolds behind my eyes. A sick glimpse into the future. I'm not going to Paris with Benny. We won't be eating at Jardin Bleu or touring the kitchen afterward. We won't be riding the train home with Benicio, playing board games in an air-conditioned compartment. We'll never again be the family we've become. The only thing left of Benny will be his chocolate fingerprints, somewhere on this train.

"We will find him," the stranger says to me. And then he takes charge, shouting down the aisle in French.

CHAPTER TWO

My mouth fills with a salty, metallic taste. "I bit my tongue," I say, aware of a shriek lingering in the dark. "Did I scream?"

Benicio sits up and peels the hair from my face. "Let me get you some water."

I reach for his hand but he's already gone. In his place, our old dog, Pinto, rises from the floor and licks my fingers.

It's been five days. A fresh dose of anguish fills my limbs. Today, of all days, is Benny's eighth birthday. I can't face the still air in the kitchen, Benny's phantom shape on his stepstool, his little boy hands orchestrating sugar, salt, herbs. "Try *this*, Mutti—"

Benicio returns, reaches for the bedside lamp.

"No," I say. "Go back to sleep."

He lowers himself onto the bed, hands me the water, and says, "I wasn't asleep."

My swallows are loud and vulgar-sounding in the dark. I set the glass on the side table, half-finished.

Three years ago to the day, in this same bed, I watched the sun crest over Fraumünster Church, reflect off its spire, and lay a gold stripe across Benicio's cheeks as he slept. I was dreading the call from Isabel. Every year it comes on Benny's birthday and never fails to confuse him, to dim the light of our celebration a little. But then Benny's big eyes appeared in the crack of the bedroom door, he burst in, all sleep smell and strawberry shampoo, dragging the floppy yellow bear he'd loved to a sheen. Suddenly Isabel's call seemed nothing more than a token, a tiny price of admission I was happy to pay.

The raw memory of this threatens to close off my throat.

"We have no choice but to get through this day, sweetheart," Benicio says.

A simple thought. A simple thing to say, and yet I can't understand where he finds the strength.

"What if he thinks we're angry with him?" I say. "What if he's worried we'll blame him for going off with a stranger?" I realize I'm digging my nails into my skull as if to rake out the misery. "It's been *five days*, Benicio," I blurt. "If it's ransom they're after, then why hasn't anyone called?"

We already know the answer. A chalky, baby-faced Swede from Interpol named Isak Larrson has explained, and re-explained, that in such cases as ours, families become more desperate the more time passes, and the more desperation, the more the payoff in the end. We could wait a week, or longer. Here in Zurich people know that seven years ago I acquired a family fortune. Of all the horrific scenarios, kidnapping for ransom is the one we pray for.

"I can't stand this, Benicio," I say, and flick on the lamp. "We need to go back to France and look for him."

Benicio shakes his head.

"We should never have listened to the police."

"Sweetheart," he says.

"No." I wave him off. "I don't want to hear it."

He and the Swede disagree with me, but I can't help thinking we should've stayed in Saint-Corbenay. Beyond that is my gut suspicion that Isabel is behind this…Yes, she's locked away in a Mexican prison, at least for a few more months. But I know what she's capable of. And unlike Jonathon, the courts in Mexico allowed her to phone Benny every year on his birthday. What else might they let her do? How much access to the outside world does she *have*?

The scar from Jonathon's knife itches my ribs. Pain wedges behind it like a tiny balloon expanding between the bones.

I press Benicio's palm to my face, feeling him cup the sharp angle of my cheek. I'm evaporating, dissolving. All I manage to keep down is broth and the spongy centers of *schwarzbrot*. The act of chewing, especially first thing each morning in that silent, awful kitchen, makes me sick to my stomach. How Benicio finds the wherewithal to eat, I have no idea.

Which of us will tell Isabel about Benny? How will we play this game? Thoughts like these continue to weave like prickly threads through my reasoning.

"Today could be the day," Benicio says. He folds his arms around me and I sense his gaze looking out beyond me. If he were facing me I could read his eyes as easily as if words were forming across their watery, bloodshot veneer. They're overwrought, as one would expect, but they're also cold, filled with an agony separate from my own. *It's your fault*, they say. *Your fault our child is gone.*

He pulls away, stands, rubbing his lower back. "I'm going to get dressed and check with Isak, in case…"

He's still within arm's reach, but the room is so saturated by stillness I feel completely alone, adrift in my own bed. Rarely do I worry over the fact that we aren't legally husband and wife—it's just a technicality, nothing that kept us from adopting Benny here in Switzerland, nothing that has kept us from being a family in the truest, deepest sense of the word. Yet, today it somehow feels like an important oversight, a failure.

In a moment, I'll crawl out from under the eiderdown, dress, halfheartedly wash my face, then join the two men in the other room. That's how it's gone each morning, but as of yesterday, the bits of information they feed me have started to seem censored. At first, I thought I was just being paranoid. But twice I caught a look exchanged between Benicio and Isak—the exact look Benicio and I give each other when we're trying to hide something from Benny. What is it they're not saying?

I watch as Benicio strolls off in the boxers he now sleeps in so he can leap from bed into action should he need to. The cut of his back stirs something in me, memories of the pleasure he's brought me over the years. He once danced naked across this floor, bumping and grinding to a Spanish song on the radio, calling out, "*Caliente!,*" winking and flinging air-kisses at me. Benicio is the funniest man I've ever known. It's not hard to imagine how good he was at stand-up, decades ago in LA. The first time we kissed, we knew our lives could end any moment at the hand of Isabel or his cousin Leon, yet we laughed so hard the cackling devolved into a weepy gulping for air. Of course, it *wasn't* the last time, but the possibility amplified our senses, and that heightened state became our standard in the years that followed. I'm still so *attracted* to him, the grace of his body, the scent of his smooth caramel skin.

I squeeze the eiderdown as he crosses the room, wanting to say, "Come back to bed, love," as if nothing has changed…but everything has, and I'm appalled at myself for this moment of yearning.

Benicio lifts his clothes from the chair by the window. Behind him, dawn has finally broken, smoky and red, as he slides into his jeans.

"I'll start the coffee," he says and turns for the door, T-shirt in hand, as if he can't bear my eyes on him a second longer.

CHAPTER THREE

Later that afternoon, I'm hunched over my dining room table turned Interpol office, obsessively rereading the written statement I gave Inspector Moreau and his underling. I refuse to stop searching for the tiny forgotten detail. *Rundown*, the mysterious Frenchman had said. Why had that stuck in my ear? Once the questioning began—on the platform beneath the Saint-Corbenay sign—he managed to disappear. No one remembers seeing him walk off or reboard after the air-conditioning was fixed. Now, like everyone else on the train that day, he's a suspect too.

His description given by a witness closely matches what I saw, though hers has more detail. Mid to late thirties, lean, tall, wearing faded jeans and a fitted short-sleeved khaki shirt. Clean-shaven. Brown, sad-looking eyes. He'd rested a hand on the seat in front of her and she'd seen how rough it looked, the nails chewed or chipped, a stain of something dark beneath them. But it was his wristwatch that had drawn her attention—a silver Bulova on a black leather band, the same watch her late husband had worn. She'd caught herself staring, she said, thinking of him. The report ends with her name, Helena Watson, sixty-five, a Brit living in the sixth arrondissement of Paris.

I read, for a second time, the transcript from the hypnotist, and once more I'm frustrated not to find anything I hadn't already told Inspector Moreau in the *Post de Police* in Saint-Corbenay. "Madame Hagen, please say again why you shut the water off?" he asked me, repeatedly, and by then it was nearly three hours since Benny had vanished. Moreau's slack shoulders and thick knuckles were at odds with his nearly unmarked face, making his age hard to figure. Late thirties, forty at the outside. One after another, he let his cigarettes burn unattended across the cramped room. What could I say about shutting off the running faucet? A mother's instinct, the need for order? Only one thing is certain—Benny had been in that washroom shortly before me. By turning off the faucet, I'd smeared his fingerprints beneath my own, making it seem like I'd taken him there to wash his hands. Moreau paced, his black boots clumping. "But you said you were in the café looking for napkins?" He produced a flat smile. "I'm just trying to understand. For the sake of your Benjamin."

Two days later he sent us home without Benny.

I hug my arms around myself, catch the stale sweaty smell of unwashed skin, and recoil. I'm thinking again of the too-sweet scent hovering above the sink on the train. *Gardenias*?

I gaze up toward our lofty, seventeenth-century ceiling, as if the baroque sconces and curly leafed adornments have something to tell me about my son's whereabouts. The snow-white walls, the sculpted panels like cake frosting—this house has brought us so much happiness. I love being here more than any destination I can dream up. Before last week, its rooms were infused with *Liebe und Glück*. Love and Luck. You could feel it the instant you stepped through the door. Everyone said so. And now, it's as if everything good has been sucked, abruptly, out through the French doors, vanished forever. All I can think is that I cannot bear being here without Benny. At this hour, his birthday cake should be the centerpiece of this table. Swiss meringue drizzled with semisweet chocolate, layer upon layer of berries and Chantilly cream. The room should be full of clamoring voices; we should all be singing, clapping hands as Benny rips open gifts. *Why*, I think, *why did I indulge him with a trip to France?* I shake my head. Of all the questions we're left with, this is the only one with an easy answer.

The table's strewn with paper scraps, timelines, maps, scribbled notes on pages torn from a legal tablet. If only I could lay it all out in the proper order I might be able to spot what I'm otherwise blind to. But my mind won't settle down; I see Benny everywhere in this big house, dashing past with the dog, stopping for hugs, rattling around in the kitchen…

The phone rings for what must be the twentieth time that day, jerking me back to the here and now. It's already three in the afternoon. I lean forward to see Benicio in the front room picking up on the third ring as Isak has instructed. "Hallo, Gabi," he says. "*Ja. Ein bisschen.*" A girl from school, no doubt asking if Benny's feeling better. I wonder if the parents see through Benicio's cover story that Benny's down with chicken pox. Most don't vaccinate for it here, and Benicio's had entire conversations about Benny's condition, patiently listened to advice on itching and fever, and quoted Benny's supposed comments from his sickbed. Only one sharp mother had said she thought Benny already had the chicken pox in Kindergarten. Not missing a beat, Benicio told her that although rare, a person could get it more than once. Amazing, how easily these fabrications come to him.

We do what we're told, yet I'm filling with the wild urge to scream: *No, you're wrong, we need to call a press conference and get Benny's photo on every TV screen in Europe*. I haven't even told Klarissa, my cousin Emil's wife, who's become, in recent years, my closest friend in Zurich. She and Emil lived in New York City, he a software engineer, she an environmental lawyer. She's smart, quick, acerbic, funny. I want so badly to hear her voice, to laugh with her over coffee. Having money now, and a certain fame as a writer, has made me cautious about who I spend time with, but Klarissa's like a sister to me, and she thinks we're in Paris. Not being able to tell her the truth adds another layer to the suffering…plus, Emil's daughter Sophie is like a sister to Oliver, and he's under the same gag order. It seems absurd to think we can't trust them, but the risk is too great, so we've been told. All of this secrecy has set me to pacing, kneading my arms, gulping down tears in the bathroom. I have a vision of Benny tied up in front of a television while one of his abductors flips through news channels and finds no mention of him. How easy it would be to convince a child his age, no matter how mature, that his parents never loved him. Especially when they aren't his "real" parents. *See? No one is looking for you. Don't you know how much trouble you were? They only pretended to love you. They never wanted you to begin with. Why do you think your mother abandoned you on the train? It was so I could take you off her hands.* This is the bitter pill Interpol has made us swallow. If Benny *is* being held for ransom, publicizing his disappearance will only complicate matters. The kidnappers might simply "rid themselves" of Benny and find another target. But what if he *wasn't* taken for ransom? And what if it wasn't Isabel or Jonathon? I have to reel my mind back from the darker possibilities. The steamy taste of vomit rises to my throat. I stiffen, and wait for it to pass.

Benicio hangs up the phone and I wander into the front room and sit across from him and Isak. No one speaks. We hear the murmured conversation and momentary laughs of the other investigators, eating takeout at the kitchen counter. The smell of warm soy sauce drifts toward us. Time feels heavy, resistant to moving. Oliver is due on the four o'clock flight from JFK. Isak wouldn't even allow us to tell *him* until yesterday, and only then because I threatened to do it anyway.

And so we wait.

I study the room, trying to see it as Oliver will for the first time in five months. Something seems *off*. Maybe it's just having strangers come in and out with their paraphernalia, moving chairs around, and so on. But I notice that several of the family photos on the long south wall of the room are askew. Most are of the four of us—Benicio, Oliver, Benny, and me—the rest are my Swiss relatives whom, before seven years ago, I didn't even know I had. One of the Interpols could've brushed against them, or it could've been Benny, heavy in thought, running a finger along the wall. There's something haphazard-looking about them, as if they were taken down then put back carelessly, out of order perhaps. But when I get up and straighten them, I can't decide *what* the order was, and I sit down again, more frustrated than before.

When I think of all the years leading up to last week, how I led an utterly different life, it seems strange beyond words. I always woke charged with energy, closed myself in my office with its walls of books and big leafy plants at the windows, and wrote. If I gazed out, there was the Limmat River, the cobbled, winding streets of Old Town, and farther off, the snowcapped Alps. I sometimes lay on the woolly rug in front of the fire, reading with a child's dreamy absorption. That heavenly space has been a place to make love too—Benicio surprising me with kisses behind my ear, trailing down my throat. It's there I wrote every word of *Illume*, which, amazingly, lingered for years on best-seller lists, convincing me the next novel would be even better. Yet weeks before Benny's disappearance, the novel I've been working on had come to feel a little doomed. Why was that? And now, I can't imagine writing another sentence.

Isak steadily flips through his folder. Benicio scrolls through his cell phone. I'm empty-handed and draw my feet beneath my thighs on the sofa. I watch the two of them and know instinctively that they're up to something. Either trying to protect me from an awful truth, or quietly assembling a case against me. I can hardly blame them for thinking, *How do you lose a child on a train?* After Lyon, when the air-conditioning failed, the heat had made everyone bad tempered and self-absorbed. A few remembered me looking for Benny, but no one really remembered Benny. Of course, he'd been there. No doubt about that. Fingerprints on the faucet. His, then mine. But when were they put there?

Pinto springs up, barking, and there, suddenly, is Oliver.

A five-month absence seems to have sharpened his features, or perhaps his face has made its final shift into manhood. Either way, he resembles my mother and me more than ever. The gray-blue eyes and dark wavy hair he's let coil past his ears. The one-sided dimple. The pensive, anxious lines crimping the corners of his eyes—my mother's exactly.

Oliver drops his bags near the door and crosses the room to embrace Benicio and me. Then he holds me long and hard as Pinto paws her way up his thigh. He loosens his grasp, and then clutches me again. The familiar scent of his skin calls to mind his boy body, once so small I could attach him to my hip and gallop about a room. I close my eyes and breathe him in.

"Anything?" he whispers into my hair.

I gently shake my head no.

When I finally let go, we sink onto the sofa. I can't repress the morbid, guilty feeling of gratitude that he's made it this far. *Look at him*, I catch myself thinking, a grown man, a music journalist living in New York City. *Look at my twenty-four-old*—and for an instant, the world fills with order and affection.

This wasn't always the case. We've come so far since our miserable existence with Jonathon in Portland, Oregon. Oliver was a snarky, angry teenager then—my mere existence sent him up the wall. There were times I honestly believed he was lost to me, that I'd never again know Ollie, the boy whose face lit up at the sight of mine. But Oliver's difficult teenage years abruptly ended when Jonathon and Isabel turned dangerously greedy, and our lives, especially mine, were nearly lost. Getting through that time bonded us in a way nothing else could.

I squeeze his hand, take him in—the leather shoes, hair cut to give the illusion of accidentally falling into place, vintage-looking turquoise and gray plaid work shirt with white snaps, dark jeans. Under normal circumstances he'd seem handsome, happy, relaxed.

Benicio introduces him to Isak. After that, Oliver appears to study me. "You need to eat," he finally says.

I nod at the floor.

The room falls silent. Benicio rubs his eyes. Beside him, Isak buries his face in another folder. The only sound is Pinto nervously licking her paws.

"My mother told me you were looking into the several cases brought against her a few years back by people who claimed her money was somehow theirs," Oliver says to Isak. "I'm pretty sure they were all crazy. But has it turned up anything?"

Isak glares at me, clearly unhappy that I've shared this information with Oliver. "No. Nothing," he says. "Everyone appears to have gone on with their unremarkable lives. One of them is now deceased."

The silence washes back around us as we retreat into our separate thoughts. A little later, Oliver rattles around the kitchen and returns with a platter of bread, cheese, and olives for the coffee table, along with an opened bottle of red wine and four glasses. The platter is Italian, white ceramic…the same one Benny used for his soft pretzels stuffed with peach marmalade and cream cheese. His two front teeth were loose and the pretzels were easy to chew. At the sight of it, I nearly smell the beer batter, the salt and yeast, hear Benny saying *Check it!*—an expression picked up from Oliver—as he held one out to me.

Oliver passes me a chunk of Brie-smeared schwarzbrot. His hand trembles. He pours me wine. Our eyes meet and his mouth curls into a mournful smile.

“Thank you,” I whisper. My mouth fills with the buttery-mushroom taste of the cheese, then the bite of the zinfandel. I realize how thirsty I've been. The wine goes down like water.

There's been no call for ransom, and—equally disturbing—no morning call from Isabel.

“Have you talked to Willow?” Oliver asks me.

I shake my head. “I'm not allowed.” I glance at Isak. “Besides, she has enough to worry about. Running the hotel, taking care of the kids.”

Willow and I have been close for years—she owns the small hotel in Mismaloya, Mexico, where I hid from Jonathon and Isabel, and later she helped me escape to Switzerland. She's come to Zurich often, but since she married a widower two years ago, adopting his three children, I've barely seen her.

“What's new since we talked?” Oliver asks.

“They dredged a lake outside Saint-Corbenay,” I blurt, but instantly regret it. “I'm sorry,” I say. “I didn't mean to sound so…I don't know.”

Isak carefully places his elbows on his knees, one then the other, letting the folder dangle. "We're now certain the wiring in the train's air-conditioning unit was cut," he says.

"At the stop in Lyon?" Oliver asks.

"It would appear so."

"Wouldn't it have to be someone who worked on the train?" I ask.

"Not necessarily," Isak says. "You have to keep in mind there were hundreds of passengers, many foreign. It takes time to investigate such a list, getting their governments to cooperate. But of course, yes, we've been questioning the train personnel, conducting background checks. So far, nothing unusual."

"Why aren't there cameras on these trains?" Oliver asks.

Isak gives us a look tinged with chagrin. "It would cost millions," he says.

I turn to Oliver and say, "I want to go back and look for Benny myself, but Isak keeps…advising against it."

"What mother *wouldn't* want to do this?" Isak says. I notice for the first time how greasy his hair is, how the skin around his nose is shiny, unwashed. "But, as I've explained, you'd only be a distraction. Too much can go wrong."

"It's been *five days*," I say. "You're no closer to finding him, as far as I can see. Unless you're not telling me something."

"Celia," Benicio says, his tone suggesting that I'm becoming a problem. "They can't share every lead."

I stare back, then recall the moment we locked eyes on the platform. His look of terror, the way we searched each other's faces, unable to speak as the horror engulfed us. It was the moment our solid life began to unravel. And now, again, the two of us eye to eye, I feel another rip.

Oliver suddenly steps in and offers to go to France with me. I turn sharply. I haven't considered this, but I see at once that it's a great idea. He is, after all, a journalist, knowing how to ask the right questions, and, beyond that, there's no way Benicio will agree to go with me, and I could use the company.

"There's nothing to indicate Benny is *in* Saint-Corbenay now," Isak says.

"Then what does it matter if I go there?" I say, wanting to blunt the impact of what he's implied—that Benny could be *anywhere.*

Isak frowns. "We can't have you compromising..."

I've stopped listening. I always imagined Interpol as a creature with far-reaching tendrils, capable of rescuing anyone, neutralizing anything in its path. The idea that my presence could foul up their entire investigation leaves me shaken, leaves me with an image of Interpol as nothing more than a troop of Keystone Kops. I know this is wrong. It's ignorant of me to think such things, and yet I can't help it, I can't move past the feeling that Benny will never be found if I don't look for him myself.

Energy jolts my legs when I stand. I picture a map of Europe, all the countries, cities, rivers, lakes, oceans, and seas. Benny is somewhere on that map, and sitting here isn't going to bring him home. "You tell me you have leads," I say, "but not what they are or whether they actually *amount* to anything."

"I understand how you must feel," Isak says.

"*Really*?" I say.

I see Benicio edging forward in his chair, getting ready to pacify me.

Isak rubs a hand across his face. "There's nothing so terrible as this, a child taken," he says.

"What's your *success* rate in cases like this?"

He stares back in frustration. "It does no good to compare cases," he says. "Each one—" Benicio stands and gently takes my arm. "Celia, it's hard on everyone. This isn't helping."

I knock his hand away and turn to Isak. The wine brings a glassy smoothness to my gestures, a certainty to my voice. "You're here to watch me, aren't you?"

Until now, this thought was barely a wisp of a suspicion, but all at once, I know it's true, and so does Benicio—again his face betrays him. Only Oliver appears confused.

I stop Isak before he has a chance to speak.

"Excuse me," I say, "but fuck you, Isak."

"*Mom*," Oliver says.

"Please," Isak says. "Please sit down so we can discuss this."

Benicio is silent.

"There are certain aspects to this case, certain factors that may have influenced..." Isak goes on.

I glare at Benicio and know instinctively that these "factors" are what they were discussing behind my back this morning.

"Benicio told me about the novel you're writing," Isak says.

Heat pools in my stomach.

"What novel?" Oliver asks.

I glare at Benicio.

"Mom. What's he talking about?"

"Celia," Benicio says, his voice soft and familiar again, bringing a split second of relief to my gut. "Look. He asked me about the days leading up to the trip. What you were doing. What *I* was doing."

"No one's accusing you of anything," Isak says. "I only want you to tell me who could've known you were writing such a book. Did you consult anyone?"

"*What* novel?" Oliver insists, standing.

I reach for his hand and cover my eyes with my other arm. I tell myself not to cry and after a moment I know I won't. But when I open them, I see Benny's red sneakers by the door—as shocking as a pool of blood—and have to catch myself on Oliver's shoulder. He eases me back down to the sofa.

"I'm writing a story based loosely on what happened to you and me," I say then. "But I made up the boy, he's *imaginary*. It's what I *do*, Oliver." Out of the corner of my eye, I see a twitch in Benicio's mouth. "Don't you dare look at me like that, Benicio." I'm now up on my feet again.

"I'm not looking at you like anything," he says.

"I told no one about the novel but you," I say.

Isak says, "Not your agent?"

"Why are you *asking* me this? Do you actually think someone learned I was writing a novel about a missing child then stole my son? Life imitating art? That's crazy."

"It's not always clear what goes on in the minds of others."

"Why don't you just come out and say you think I'm involved."

"Celia," Benicio says. "Back off. We're all upset. Isak just wants to—"

"Then why hasn't he asked us the *right* questions, about your sister? Why hasn't he asked you what you've told her?"

Benicio cuts his eyes at me.

"For the first time in seven years Isabel hasn't called on the morning of Benny's birthday," I say. "Now why is that, Benicio? Did you tell her he's not here? Why else would she not call?"

"I have no idea," Benicio says, straight-faced. "I haven't talked to her."

"You're *lying*," I say, suddenly sure this is true. I turn to Isak. "He's lying about something," I say. "Go ahead, ask him about his *sister*."

"My sister's in prison. She had nothing to do with this!"

Isak puts his hand up like a stop sign. "Yes, this has been checked," he says. "We've confirmed that she hasn't been released."

"It doesn't matter," I say. "Has anyone kept track of who she communicates with and how?"

Isak doesn't answer.

In the silence that follows, I'm sure what I have to do. I already see the linden trees and arched stone windows, big enough for a person to crouch inside, the Dutch bikes with their worn wicker baskets, the ornate iron light fixtures looping above doorways, lit in the night fog where a child snatcher is on the loose. I feel my hands squeezing into icy fists.

Someone speaks but I'm no longer listening. I know exactly which clothes to pack, which shoes are best for walking on uneven cobbles. I'll bring my old Thermos and fill it with water to stay hydrated in the heat. Sunglasses. A straw hat. Remember to wear a watch. Take notes. Ride that goddamn train as many times as it takes to figure out where to stash a child. "Celia!" Benicio's voice cuts in. I come around with the woozy feel of having passed out. But I'm still on my feet. Everyone is still in place.

"Did you hear a word I said?"

"It's the wine," I say, waving him off.

When I lift my head again, I see tears in Oliver's eyes.

I reach out toward him, but there's the white platter with crumbs and a few crumbles of cheese and I think of Benny's loose teeth again and wonder if they've fallen out, and whether he even has a pillow to put one under, and it's this last thought that breaks me. I grip the platter by the handles, bring it down, and snap it over my knee, letting the two halves clunk to the rug.

"Oh god," I say.

Everyone is staring at me now, including the agents from the kitchen.

After a long moment, Benicio kneels by me and picks up the china pieces and takes them away without a word.

And only after he has returned, handed me a tumbler of water, and dabbed at my pant leg with a damp cloth, does Oliver come and sit on the coffee table facing me. He takes one of my hands in both of his and flicks a quick look up at Isak. "Benicio says Interpol thinks there was a man on the train who might've taken an interest in Benny."

I feel a low shudder in my heart. "It's someone who works for Isabel, isn't it?" I say.

"Please," Benicio says. "Enough about Isabel."

"Then what are you *saying*?"

"The man who helped you look for Benny on the train," Isak says. "Are you sure you've never seen him before?"

I look at him in total confusion.

"I'm asking if you're sure you've never seen him. He's not someone you know?"

"Someone I *know*?"

Isak glances at Benicio. Benicio looks at the floor and chews the inside of his lip.

"What's going *on* here?" I say.

Isak opens the folder in his lap and hands me a grainy eight-by-ten photograph. "This is from the security camera at the Zurich Hauptbahnhof."

How long has Isak been sitting on this? The folder he's pulled it from appears to have been in his hand most of the day. Why show this to me *now*?

My breath comes in heaving gulps at the sight of Benny. I clutch my sweater to my throat and stare at the black-and-white image of us boarding the train. My foot on the first step, my mouth open in laughter, head tossed slightly back as I hoist up our bag. My free hand is clasped in Benny's behind me. He's laughing too, dangling the picnic basket, his chunky backpack drooping from his shoulders. But his face is turned, tilted up toward the man behind him. *A man in a khaki shirt and jeans. Silver wrist-watch with a black leather band.* A man without luggage. Empty hands. *Rough hands. Chewed or chipped nails. A stain of some sort beneath them.* The man who asked for a rundown of what Benny was wearing had already known. He's sharing a laugh with my son. And, it appears, he's sharing a laugh with me.

CHAPTER FOUR

I have no explanation. All I have is the truth and it's winning over no one. I wasn't paying attention. It's that simple. Benny was chattering on about a concoction of his, a combination of unlikely spices so silly it made him laugh.

"What distracted you?" Isak asks.

I flip the photograph onto the coffee table, unable to bear the sight of his joyful face. Things are looking worse than ever for me. The longer I take to respond, the more implicated I seem, yet my mouth refuses to open. Then it occurs to me that I don't *have* to tell him the rest of the truth, don't need to make myself look more pathetic by admitting that I was obsessing about my novel, the one he'd already suggested might've played some bizarre role in Benny's disappearance. I'm not about to tell him how self-absorbed I was that morning, fearful that the wall I'd hit would prove to be a permanent barrier between the page and me. Nor do I intend to explain how, over the previous weeks, I'd grown increasingly annoyed with both the novel and all the attention Benny seemed to require of me.

"I'm sorry," I say. "I spend a lot of time inside my own head. I can't tell you what I was thinking that moment."

Nothing I say will loosen his jaw.

Everyone waits.

"Do I need a *lawyer*?" I ask.

"Celia—" Benicio says.

I turn and run upstairs, where I lock my office door behind me and collapse at my desk. As far as I know, I've not been followed. I stare down at the Limmat River swirling a blue ribbon through the center of town. The sidewalks on either side pulse with people, surely in good spirits on this summer's day, though, it occurs to me that any one of them could be behind Benny's kidnapping. *Is that how it's going to be now?* I think. *Having to question everything, taking nothing at face value?*

I think of Benny's hands steeped in dough, his green eyes intent on his task. "Black pepper," he says to himself, as if repeating something whispered in his ear. He's made ginger-snap ice cream sandwiches, and now his eyes blink at the spice on his tongue. Dabs of vanilla bean ice cream ooze from the corners of his mouth. "My other *mamá* says spicy food is my other *papá's* favorite," he says. Then I see him on our rooftop terrace, plucking chervil from the small greenhouse. Pigeons look on from the copper gutter. Benny holds up the lacy herb, gives it a shake. "Looks like carrot tops," he says. A moment later, he gets an odd, serious look. "Which direction is the Gefängnis Zurich from here?" he asks, scanning the skyline to the east. I stand so quickly the pigeons flee.

I turn on the computer and, before my thoughts smother me, open the file of my novel-in-progress. Maybe Isak's not so wrong about the book. It feels like a curse I've brought down on our home. I picture myself flinging its pages into the fireplace, watching them ignite and shrivel into scrolls of black ash. But all I can do in the real world is click delete.

The computer doesn't trust me: *Are you sure? It cannot be retrieved.*

I click OK and the file is gone.

What Benny had wanted to know was where Jonathon was, which direction exactly. I've never told anyone, but twice I rode past the prison on the tram, then, a third time, I got off at Badernestrasse and went the rest of the way on foot. It was like a castle embedded in a city block, surrounded by bakeries, restaurants, an eye doctor, an *Apotheke*. The normalcy of it all hit me like a sucker punch to the throat. This ornate, academy-style prison with its turret and white-paned windows was deemed suitable punishment for a man who'd had me kidnapped and tortured, who'd shoved a knife between my ribs with his own hand. I'd stood outside in my long overcoat and scarf, just staring, my insides searing with rage. I imagined Jonathon peering out to people-watch. Jonathon with sun on his face. Jonathon's heart touched by the first snowfall of the year. And, as if that weren't enough, a gate on a side street let me see into the prison courtyard where a silver sculpture, spiked like a teepee of sticks for kindling, cast the sun upward to the barred windows. In between writing appeals, Jonathon could contemplate art.

After deleting the novel in my office, I somehow ended up in my bedroom in bed. An hour later I'm still there, whispering a prayer to the ceiling, waiting out the twilight of Benny's birthday.

And then, Benicio's standing over me, though it's unclear for how long. Pinto leaps near my feet, circles, then draws her chin down and drapes her ears across my ankle. She drifts off, her eyebrows continuing to twitch. Through the half-closed curtains, the sky is plum colored; stringy clouds tear apart in the wind. The heat is coming to an end. I'll wake to morning rain.

"You must remember something else about laughing with Benny," Benicio says finally.

I'm thinking of the witness again, Helena Watson, her calling the mystery man's eyes sad. I'd looked into his stare, there in the aisle—he seemed to know all about the panic surging in my chest.

"You were *laughing* at something," Benicio says.

I will myself to recapture the faces of strangers, to pick out the one tracking Benny and me, studying us, calculating. But it's no use. I can't remember what I didn't see. I was thinking about the heat, about the novel crumbling. All those months gone, wasted. "Benicio," I say, gathering myself, "I had a hold of his hand when we got on. I wasn't careless." I am unsure if this is true.

"No, of course not," he answers, "but what were you laughing at?"

"I'm telling you *I don't remember*. Just because a camera recorded my face that split second doesn't mean I know what I was thinking. Tell me what *you* were thinking when you scratched your head in the living room two hours ago. I took your picture, you want to see it?"

Benicio's heavy sigh flutters the thin hairs on my arm.

The thing I won't say is this: With school out for summer, Benny has needed so much of my time. While other kids from his school are off at camp, he's home in the kitchen, if not cooking, then making lists, experimenting with oils, fruits, French herbs and mushrooms found only at the farmer's market across town. While other boys build Lego towers, Benny handles razor-sharp knives, boils water, adjusts gas burners. We could have hired more help, a nanny even. But early on we agreed that we'd take care of him ourselves. He might grow up in an estate but the values of our family would remain simple, hands-on, and that included making sure the boys did chores. I didn't want them believing someone else should do their laundry. I've wanted them—*all of us*—to be self-reliant. But there's no denying I have trouble trusting strangers. Who wouldn't under the circumstances? Aside from young cousins babysitting for an evening out, and another set of cousins, Claudia and Renata, whose housecleaning business brings them over twice a week, and whom Isak has already checked out under the guise of government auditors, we've always managed for ourselves.

But he's only seven years old—*eight*. His hands are small and not completely under his control. Over the years Benicio and I have supervised him more or less equally, but lately Benicio's been traveling, consulting on one film then another, researching in Paris for his new screenplay. In just the last three months, he's been to LA four times. We've lost our balance.

Benicio drags the reading chair to the side of the bed. He faces me as if visiting a sick patient.

"Sweetheart," he says.

"Something's wrong with the portraits in the living room," I say.

Benicio leans in and takes my hand between both of his. I smell celery on his breath, the citrusy fragrance of his shampoo. He's eaten, he's showered—his hair's still wet. When did he manage *that*? Time's not working the way it's supposed to.

"I thought maybe some were knocked down and put back up," I say. "Maybe Benny—? I don't know. What order were they in?"

After a moment I realize that what I think is Benicio's caress of my hand is actually the shuddered rhythm of his tears.

I sit up and pull him toward me. His cool damp hair clings to my cheek. I rub his back as if in a daydream, his T-shirt warm and cotton soft beneath my palm, my fingers bumping down his spine. But his agony presses against me like a hot blanket I suddenly have the urge to shove from my skin.

"I love you," he whispers into my neck.

I tell him I love him too, and for an instant the feeling is the same as always—a slow heat radiating across my chest. But it's no longer all there is; mistrust rushes to its side like a menacing twin.

"I'm sorry," he says.

I'm about to say there's no need for apology. I'm about to ask, *What do you have to be sorry for?* I'm about to ask, *What could you have possibly done?* when he puts his mouth on mine and straddles me on the bed.

"Not *now*," I say, against his mouth, but already I'm kissing him, hard. I have the urge to punish him, punish myself—for losing our child, for indulging in this, for *needing* this. Benicio's tears are wet on my mouth. I dig my nails into his back. We are poachers, taking what doesn't belong to us, stealing a comfort we don't deserve. We are ugly, crying, grunting, enduring the very thing that used to bring us joy.

CHAPTER FIVE

Benicio slumps into the chair by the bed, and I melt across the covers. The sun weakens, then disappears. We're dressed again, but thrown like wreckage, adrift. When a knuckle raps the door I welcome the intrusion. "Come in," I say, expecting Oliver.

Inspector Moreau stands in the doorway, his face eerily shadowed by the overhead light. A moan erupts from my throat. Pinto barks and lunges; she's used to strangers in the house, but not in the bedroom. I manage to catch hold of her collar.

Benicio spins in his chair.

Gone is Moreau's powder-blue polo tucked into pressed pants tucked into combat boots. Gone the blue cap with gold piping. His short hair lies flat, as if lacquered to his skull. His white shirtsleeves are rolled neatly to his elbows. His cologne leads the way as he crosses the room toward us.

I can't make sense of Moreau being here. Is he off duty? Off the *case*? Has he hand-carried news of Benny because it's too grim for the telephone? Or does he mean to *arrest* me? I feel, suddenly, like I'm dropping through space, accelerating. I squeeze Pinto against me and her bark dwindles to a low growl.

"May I?" Moreau says, of the empty chair against the wall.

A rational corner of my mind tells me the buzzing sensation I feel is shock. I'm going into shock.

"Yes, of course." Benicio drags the chair to the bed, then Moreau sits so that both men are now facing me.

"May I?" Moreau says again, reaching for the bedside lamp.

Benicio nods and a cone of yellow light spreads across his face, revealing speckles of whiskers.

Pinto sniffs the air, still doubtful. I slide beneath the eiderdown and gather her close again. Seven happy years in this house. Extraordinary years. After having come so close to death, and then dodging it so magnificently, these years have been such a gift.

Don't say it, I think. *Don't make it real.*

"I'm sorry," Moreau says. His eyes are the color of chestnuts, and round, too, like chestnuts, but since I saw him, just days ago, the rims have turned an ashy blue, the lines around his mouth have deepened into ridges.

A droning white silence whirls between the walls.

"But we haven't found your Benjamin," he says.

Haven't found your Benjamin.

Air bursts from my lips.

"I have a few more questions, and thought it best to come in person. As *myself*. As a father, a grandfather. Separate from Inspector Moreau."

These words flood me with relief.

And disbelief. And dread.

Moreau is in my bedroom, five hundred and sixty kilometers from Saint-Corbenay. Which means Benny is still missing, still out in the world needing to be found. I struggle to grasp what's happening. Is this a tactic to make me lower my guard, admit something, incriminate myself? Do they honestly think I could have done something to Benny? In a flash I see the turret, the sculpture, the white-paned windows of Jonathon's prison.

"May I smoke?" Moreau asks.

Benicio reaches for the water glass from the bedside table and hands it to Moreau for an ashtray. Moreau stares inside and sloshes the bit of water as if stalling to form his thoughts before he speaks.

He lights the Gauloise pinched between his lips and draws on it, quickly. "I have seen the photograph," he says, expelling the tarry smoke sideways. "They faxed it to me this morning."

So that's it. Isak has had the photograph the entire day, if not longer. It's possible he showed it to Benicio before I even got out of bed this morning.

"Curious," Moreau says. "That this man should be right behind you. Laughing. Then offering to help find the boy. Then vanishing himself."

"No kidding," I say. "But if you're asking for some kind of explanation from me, save your breath."

Moreau simply stares at me, noncommital.

Finally, he gives the tiniest of nods, and says, "You know, I love the movies."

Out of the corner of my eye, I see Benicio's arms tightening against his chest.

Moreau draws again on his cigarette, then taps the ash into the glass, where it sizzles in the water. "Especially the old detective films. *Films noirs.* A bit of a cliché, I suppose. But I could spend all of a Saturday watching these films. Sadly, my favorite series has never been translated into French so I watch in English. Inspector Stark. British. You know it perhaps?" He looks back and forth between us. "In any case," he adds, "I've sharpened my English on these films."

"Please," Benicio says, "say what you have to say."

But just then Isak pops his head in the doorway. "How is everything?" he asks.

Moreau offers Isak a tight-lipped smile, and I sense that a turf war's about to break out, each of them believing he could crack the case, if the other would only clear out of the way.

But, for now, Isak narrows his eyes, nods, and disappears.

Moreau turns to Benicio with a strange look—surprise, giving way, oddly, to pity. The look he gives me, I can't read at all. "The man on the train wanted a 'rundown' of what your Benjamin was wearing," he says. "Is this right?"

"*Yes*," I say. "We've been through all that."

Moreau nods without taking his eyes off me. "It's just that it sounds so much like Inspector Stark: *Let's get a rundown on that guy*."

"Didn't I say that when we first talked—that his words sounded like they had quotes around them?" But now I'm wondering if I only thought this.

"I have a child of my own," he says after a moment. "A girl close in age to your Benny." His cigarette is burning down, untouched, the ash about to fall in his lap.

"OK," I say.

He nods. "I'm very protective of her."

And I'm *not* protective of Benny? Is that what he means? Is this the message everyone wants to give me, that even if I'm not behind all this, I'm still guilty, still a poor excuse for a mother? I rub the raw edge of my bitten tongue against my teeth. He has no idea how *overprotective* I am, how suspicious of others. He doesn't know how I've had to *train* myself not to see threats everywhere, not to deny the boys room to grow.

"To find your son," Moreau says, "is to save my own daughter. Do you see?"

Another dramatic pull on his cigarette, and the ash falls, miraculously into the glass. He's blowing smoke around, gesturing as if he has all the time in the world. "Your son disappeared in Saint-Corbenay, as you know. Not only is this village my district, it's my *ville natale*, my place of birth, and where I live now, with my wife and daughter, Arabelle."

Benicio glances at me, his face drained of patience.

"And, you see, Arabelle was approached not long ago by a strange man."

Benicio and I both sit up straighter. "He asked her questions about who she was and where her parents were. He had a strange accent, she said. And he frightened her. She had the good intelligence to run home. This was six months ago. Saint-Corbenay is a small town, but I no longer know everyone who lives there. Roma Gypsies pass through, wealthy foreigners acquire old properties and renovate them for profit. We have a couple of hotels, two bed-and-breakfasts. Tourists hiking in and out. So, no, I don't know who this man was. I never saw him before in Saint-Corbenay. I have not seen anything of him since. Until, perhaps, now."

My skin prickles.

"And you say you didn't know this man on the train, the man who wanted *a rundown*?"

"No. I keep telling you."

He stares at me another moment, as if trying to decide how far to push. "Yet he made you laugh," he says.

"He did *not* make me laugh. I realize that's what it looks like in the photo, but it's an illusion. Benny and I were just…getting on the train. I explained all this to Isak."

"You really have no idea who this man is?" Benicio asks Moreau. "No clue where he came from?"

"Ah," Moreau says, releasing another gust of tar from the side of his mouth. "This is the essential question."

He pauses to rub his temple with a force that reddens the skin. And then he nods deeply, as if under the weight of something he'd rather not put into words. "As our Cockney inspector would say, 'This is the 'ole inta which everything 'as fallen.'"

CHAPTER SIX

Why do I feel this is all a ruse? Or just another stray fact, nothing at all to do with Benny?

Moreau lifts a single eyebrow as he crushes his unfinished cigarette against the inside of the glass. "It can be hard to think clearly when a thing so dreadful has happened. Difficult to locate a fact inside one's own head." He taps his temple. "But I believe it is only a matter of allowing it to come to the surface."

So this is how the French solve a crime, I think. Don't rack your brains over it, just let the truth bob up out of the murk.

"I'm *sorry*," I say. "My son is missing, I can't eat, I can't sleep. You must know I've gone through every damn second of that day over and over—"

"Madame Hagen, I don't doubt this."

I cross my arms, realize it makes me look defensive, and drop my hands into my lap.

Moreau's head tips to the side as if something is understood between us. I have no idea what that might be.

"Inspector," I say. "Tell me why you're here."

"As I said. To speak with you again, as a father."

Benicio leans back in his chair and links his hands behind his head. The muscles of his arms tauten, his T-shirt pulls across his muscular chest, and the contrast between his lean, sturdy build and Moreau's soft, fatigued-looking frame is a statement being shouted loud and clear. "With all due respect," Benicio says, "why come all the way to Zurich to sit in our bedroom and ask the same questions Isak has asked a dozen times?"

Moreau spins the glass with the tips of his fingers, like a blind man attempting to read a face. "*D'accord*," he says at last. "Let's… travel in another direction."

He turns to me.

"But before we chase that rabbit through *la forêt*, have I told you I've been married to the unapologetic Madame Moreau for twenty years?"

When Benicio and I fail to respond, he goes on, "It is true. Twenty years, as of one month ago. And did I say that in France she is quite a well-known painter?"

"And what does she paint that she needs to apologize for?" Benicio asks in a voice that makes clear he's playing along with nonsense.

"Madame Moreau paints landscapes," he says. "Fields of lavender and cliffs, for instance. But they are not the pretty countrysides one's *grand-mère* would hang above the buffet. Madame Moreau's paintings are more abstract, more, let us say, unusual." He can't seem to keep his lips from producing a small, private grin. "*Non*, not for rooms where one wishes to have polite conversation. An English critic once called them 'ribbons of human forms cutting through the ragged cliffs of Provence.' The human forms are in various states of…grace, if you will. They sell for very fine sums, which is a fine thing for a man on a French gendarme's salary."

"Inspector," Benicio says.

"Ah, *pardon. Oui*, the point. It's getting late. The *unapologetic* refers to *une liaison* she had with a young sculptor. Ten years ago now."

I feel myself recoil even as I silently do the math. Moreau's wife must be about forty. Ten years ago she would have been thirty, her sculptor perhaps twenty?

"He was a student of hers. What a meal for the public. They ate and they ate of it."

I'm fascinated now, despite myself.

I hear Benicio fidgeting. As he shifts his weight, the spindles in his chair wince.

"No need to give all the details," Moreau says. "I will tell you, though, the worst part was thinking she intended to leave me."

His eyes latch on to mine.

All I can do is stare back, waiting,

"But then," he goes on, "after the immediate shock and anger, I saw that, in truth, I didn't care what she'd done. Frenchmen are known for taking mistresses, and had the shoe been on the other foot...well, I must confess, it *was* once, briefly. But, you see, with my wife and her young sculptor, the same people who disapproved, who felt offended, even betrayed by her...if they had known of *my* affair I felt sure they'd have asked Madame Moreau to dismiss it at once. *Pourquoi faire tout un plat?* Why the big..." He stirs up the air with his hand. "Why all the tears? No need to leave your husband over *this*."

He shrugs, looks from me to Benicio and back again, then says, "I fancy myself a modern man, unchained to the old ways. I loved my wife. I love her still. And here we are, years later, we've built a life, we have our daughter. I am still happily married to the unapologetic Madame Moreau, and she is still happily married to me."

"*Fantastique*," Benicio says.

Moreau ignores the sarcasm. "Madame Hagen, you remind me a great deal of my wife. A beautiful, brilliant success. If I may say so."

For the first time since Benny disappeared, I hear myself laugh, though it's more of a surprised bark.

"You must attract many kinds of people to you," Moreau says. "May I ask you, is it possible, in the last few months, that you met someone new?"

My face hardens. "I meet new people all the time."

"*Bien sûr.* But, you see, I'm speaking now about someone you took a special liking to, someone you had a special fondness for—"

"This sounds like an accusation," I say.

"*Non*. Certainly not."

"It's ridiculous. I'm sorry."

"So the answer is no?"

"For god's sake," I say.

Benicio edges forward, stops just short of rising, his whole face reddening.

"Understand," Moreau says, "I am trying to grasp a complete picture of your family. And by this I mean—"

"Hold *on*," I say, waving him off. "If you're asking am I having an affair with the man you think took Benny—"

"This is complicated business, Madame Hagen. Not too different from a plot in a novel, I suppose. There are threads, you see, that twist together in the most unlikely places. Surely you understand."

"*Jesus Christ,*" Benicio says, throwing his hands in the air. "Enough."

"It is not my intention to cause more pain," Moreau says.

"*Pain*? This isn't pain," I say. "This is *harassment*."

"We can't be sure that this stranger on the train took your son."

"So *I'm* still your main suspect?"

"I did not say that."

"This is so absurd. Anyone who knows me knows how much I love Benicio. You must have asked people about us."

"As you know, we wish to avoid calling attention to Benny's disappearance, but I did speak to Oliver—he assured me just how much you love your husband, Madame Hagen."

I don't bother to correct him on the technicality of marriage.

"*Oliver*?" Benicio asks. "When did you talk to Oliver?"

Before Moreau can answer, Benicio jumps back in. "No. I'm asking you to leave. You'll have to speak to our lawyer from now on."

Moreau pauses. "Very well, Monsieur Martin. But I'll be in Zurich another twenty-four hours. It shouldn't take longer than that."

"*What* shouldn't take longer than that?" Benicio asks.

I grip the pillow, ready to hurl it.

"Or perhaps less time if you'll allow me one more question? Madame Hagen?"

I hold Benicio back with one hand. "OK, what's your question?"

"I appreciate it. My question is this: Did you plan to run away with this man and your son and start a new life?"

It takes a second, but then I know, instinctively, that I'll return to this moment for the rest of my life. I'll remember the silence, so voluminous, so present. I let go of the pillow. This is what they plan to pin on me. They *never* believed a call for ransom would come. They're here to watch me, to wait for me to crack.

Moreau slowly sets his sights on Benicio while reaching to pet Pinto's head. My loyal dog leans her ear into his hand for a scratch.

I wait for Benicio to say something.

When it feels as if the string holding the entire room together is about to snap, Benicio finally opens his mouth. "Celia?" he says. "What is he talking about?"

"We know he was texting you," Moreau says. "Your phone records indicate you were sending messages about the trip, and your feelings for one another."

It's as if the breath is sucked from my chest. This can't be happening. I simply do not know the man in the photograph. Someone is *setting me up*.

Benicio thrusts himself deeper into his chair, fingers clamped on the armrests.

"He's lying, Benicio," I say. "He's screwing with us. *Someone* is screwing with us. I've never laid eyes on that man in my life."

No one seems to hear me. Moreau's gaze is fixed on Benicio with an intensity, a *menace* I haven't seen until now; Benicio is glaring straight back at him. "Monsieur Martin," Moreau finally says, "I have a question for you as well."

"No," I say. "We're done. I'm calling our lawyer."

"As you wish," Moreau says. "But I cannot leave without asking Monsieur Martin if he has shared with you how often he's been in touch with his old friend Emily."

It takes a second to register what he's said. Emily. *Emily Sandstrom?*

"This may be something to share with your lawyer as well."

I'm afraid for a moment that Benicio will lunge at Moreau.

"*Benicio.*"

He doesn't look at me.

"Honey?"

"We share the same agent," Benicio says, still glaring at Moreau.

My heart flops.

"Did you know this, Madame Hagen?"

"Wait. What did you say?" I ask Benicio.

"She and I share the same agent. It's nothing."

"Many years ago you were engaged to be married to her," Moreau says. "Is this not so?"

A suffocating silence bears down on the room. I need to get out of this bed, this house. What the hell is going on?

Moreau leans forward and places his hand atop mine.

Pinto inches deeper into my lap, and Moreau offers me a joyless smile. I glance down to see his thick, dry fingers holding my hand to the wrist. It takes a moment before I realize he's trying to steady the trembling.

CHAPTER SEVEN

One quiet evening, when Benny was nearly six, he bounced into the front room where Benicio and I were drinking wine and reading by the fire. "How did you two meet?" he asked.

I dropped my book in my lap, lowered my reading glasses, and glanced over at Benicio.

"Why are you asking?" Benicio said.

"Because I don't *know*," Benny answered.

I smiled at his logic, even as I dreaded answering the question. "What makes you ask *now* is what I think Papi means."

"Because Elisa told me her parents met on the Internet and that made them special."

"Special?" Benicio said.

Benny nodded.

"Well, hmm," Benicio said. "I think the way Mutti and I met is *far* more *interesting*."

When Benny looked away for a second, I pursed my lips, drew a line across my throat, and madly shook my head *no*.

"I was an explorer in the Mexican jungle," Benicio said, and I relaxed. "And Mutti was caught in a panther trap set by hunters, you know those giant nets that swing from a tree? I cut her down, and we lived happily ever after."

Benny took this in.

"Don't believe a word of that," I said. "*I* was the explorer, and your papi was captured by a gang of incredibly clever spider monkeys. They'd dug a hole in the ground and covered it with big branches, and he fell right in. Oh, you should have heard how he begged me to throw him a rope. It was pitiful!"

"Come on!" Benny said.

"OK," Benicio said. "I was doing gardening work at a condominium in Puerto Vallarta, and one day Mutti came there on vacation. She sat down by the pool—in one of those long chairs and she covered herself all over with smelly coconut oil…"

I raise my eyebrow at him.

"I was minding my own business, of course, working very hard, scooping bugs out of the water with a net, and trimming the camellia bushes, *snip snip*. But then, all of a sudden, she started talking to me, asking me questions—"

"Papi! You didn't do gardening work."

"No, I *did*."

I laughed. "*Schatz*, this is actually true. Well, *part* of it's true, the part where I was sitting by the pool and he was working. Then we just started talking, the way people do, and…the rest is history."

Benny narrowed his eyes, deciding whether to believe us or not.

It had been a long time since I'd thought of those first moments by the pool—hearing Benicio's work boots on the concrete apron with my eyes closed, the sound of his tools, and then hearing his voice for the first time—only hours after setting down in Mexico with Jonathon and Oliver. The real story is that I got bored with sunbathing and took out my favorite Joella Lundstrum novel, and, after a while, Benicio approached me and asked what I was reading. If the afternoon had played out even a little differently, Benny wouldn't have been there years later to ask the question of how we met. Such a flimsy thread to hang the weight of a life on. Answering Benny that day had left me with a curious longing, as if I'd lost something I was sure I hadn't lost, as if I'd caught a glimpse of all the ghostly trails leading to other outcomes. I remember being very aware, suddenly, in a gut way, that one of those alternative paths led to Emily, the woman Benicio apparently still loved at the time we met, a path no less plausible than the one leading to me. I thought of all the things Benny didn't know about us, things I prayed he'd never find out. In any case, not long after we met at the pool, Benicio and I were kidnapped, and in the long hours of waiting to learn what Isabel and their cousin Leon would do with us, we began to open up to each other. It was then I first heard of Emily.

"Long story made short," Benicio had told me, "my parents were killed when a bus they were traveling in was forced off the road into a ravine. They had debts on their property that we didn't know about. I snuck into the States to help pay them and got a job in a frozen food factory in LA. I sent every dollar home that I didn't need to survive. I'd always been the class clown, and one night at a comedy club I started to banter with a comedian on stage and it turned out I was funnier than he was. One thing led to another and I became part of the comedy scene. I even had a couple of small parts in movies you've probably never heard of."

"Try me," I said.

"*Austin's Willing Execution.*"

"A comedy?"

"Hilarious."

"Never heard of it."

"Told you. The other was *In the Company of Harold's Daughter.*"

"You were in that? My *god*. Oliver has that. He's watched it a hundred times."

"And you?" Benicio asked.

"Nope."

"I rest my case. Anyway," he continued with a smile, "I sent even more money home and after a while I figured the debts had been paid. What I didn't know was that Leon had taken some of the money and started a business on the side. You get my drift. He hired my sister. I got deported, and the rest you know."

I flipped my hand over and squeezed his fingers. My scabby, rope-scarred wrist seemed to glare up at us. "What happened to the woman you were engaged to?" I asked.

This seemed to catch him off guard. "Emily. Yes, well, Emily went on to marry a guy I did shows with. I always thought he was the one who called the INS."

"Really?"

"Yes. But the joke's on him. It doesn't pay to be a rebounder."

The word *rebounder* stuck in my head. I tried to imagine myself rebounding. There'd be issues. Serious issues. How could I ever get close to someone again? How could I ever trust anyone after this?

"Emily doesn't really care about him," Benicio said. "At least that's what she says in her e-mails."

In the quiet that followed, his face took on a raw, achy look, his eyes narrowing to slits.

Years later, on the evening Benny had asked about our meeting, he went to his first sleepover at a friend's. I remember this distinctly because Oliver had already gone off to college, and it was the first time Benicio and I had been alone in the house since Benny'd come to live with us. We went at each other crazily, like a pair of teenagers starved for privacy, desperate not to waste an instant. Yet in the midst of so much pleasure, I'd felt a trace of Emily, as if memories of her eddied around inside Benicio's mind. I couldn't will them away; instead, I started tickling Benicio. Hard, in the ribs. He twisted sideways, laughing, and I ran to our bed, where he found me with a bowler hat from a costume party, on my head. "How Milan Kundera of you," he said from the doorway, his interest in me still obvious. "How nerdish of you to point that out," I said, tipping the hat and pulling back the eiderdown where he joined me for one of the most memorable evenings we've ever shared.

CHAPTER EIGHT

Now Moreau tucks that same eiderdown around me as I shiver.

Los Angeles. Four times in the last three months.

"He's playing us," Benicio says. "Don't listen to him."

I want to follow his voice back to my heart. *You love this man deeply, fiercely*, I remind myself. Yet I ask him, "In what way have you been *in touch* with Emily?"

"He's twisting it," Benicio answers. "He wants it to look like something it's not."

Moreau seems not at all offended. He leans back, crosses his arms, studies us as if observing a surgery in progress.

"But this mystery man on the train," Benicio says. "Are you lying about *him*?"

"How can you *ask* that?"

"How can I ask? Because I don't know what to think, Celia."

Before I can say, "You *ought* to know," I catch Oliver's silhouette in the doorway—how eerily like Jonathon he looks, shoulders curled forward, fists crammed in pockets, head cocked to the side.

"Mind if I come in?" he asks.

I shoot him a forbidding look, but Moreau says, "Not at all," and Oliver enters. His stride, too, is Jonathon's.

Moreau glances at Oliver, then me, then Oliver, as if trying to intercept the thoughts zipping between us. Oliver lowers himself to the foot of the bed, and Pinto flops her head onto his lap. "Everything all *right*?" he asks.

I have to stifle a nervous, grossly inappropriate laugh.

"It's not a good time, Oliver," Benicio says.

"Has something happened? Did you find Benny?"

"No, honey, we haven't found your brother," I say, then can't keep myself from adding, "We found *Emily*. But apparently she wasn't missing after all."

"For god's sake, Celia."

I wrench the blanket off my shoulders. "Since when's she been with your *agent*?"

"A year. Something like that."

A *year.* I can't even think what to say.

"Don't you give me that look," Benicio says, bordering on furious now. "I could ask just as easily how long you've known the comedian from the train, the one who had you and Benny cracking up."

"May I say something here?" Moreau says.

"Don't you *dare,*" I tell him, then snap my head back toward Benicio. "I'm going to say this one last time. The man on the train was a complete and utter stranger. I don't understand why, but I'm being *set up.*" I grab a breath. "On the other hand, it seems pretty obvious what he's saying about you is *true.*"

"We weren't seeing each other," he says after a long moment.

"You were in touch. What does that *mean*?"

"Not what you think!"

"What going *on*?" Oliver asks.

Moreau seems just shy of amused. "Just getting some items out from the shadows."

"No, enough," Benicio says. "This is bullshit."

I throw my hand up before he says anything more. I face Moreau and say, "You're right. He was engaged to her before we met—and she kept e-mailing him long after she'd married his supposed friend. She wanted him *back*. Isn't that right, Benicio? *Tell him.*"

Benicio ignores me, takes a step in Moreau's direction instead, as if to muscle him toward the door.

Moreau gives a slightly theatrical shrug. "Monsieur, this is simply old-fashioned police work. Checking phone records, and the like."

I glare at Benicio again. "You were *calling* her?"

"No. Only…a couple of times," Benicio says.

"Quite true," Moreau says, nodding. "But a big amount of texting back and forth. Isn't this so, Monsieur?"

Benicio stands knuckling his forehead.

In an ugly flash I see Benicio and Emily reuniting—their absurd joy. "So how long have you two been *texting* each other?" I ask.

"The better part of six months," Moreau says, glancing at Benicio for confirmation.

"That's it," I say, unharnessing myself from the bed.

I bolt past Benicio and begin shoving clothes into a backpack. Pinto watches from a distance, ears and tail stiffened in fear. For five days, shock has insulated my sanity from the fiery nerves trying to set it aflame. The body's defense mechanism at work. But by now the shock has morphed into anger, and anger is a potent fuel. I will think of nothing else, *do* nothing else, until I find Benny.

Over my shoulder, I see that Moreau and Oliver have slipped out.

"Listen to me," Benicio says, as I swing the pack up onto the bathroom sink.

I slide my toothbrush into a side pouch along with a small bottle of Motrin and leave everything else. When I whip around, Benicio's body is blocking the door.

"You need to *get out of my way*," I say.

I've never spoken to him like this in all our years together. I can't believe I'm doing it now. But a horrible truth is rushing at me: I've made the same mistake twice. Trusted too easily, too *lazily*. I'd thought I'd known Jonathon through and through, but what a joke that proved to be. Afterward, I'd told myself I'd never feel so betrayed ever again, or be so seduced by denial as I was with him.

But now Benicio. *Benicio!*

"An hour ago in our bed," I say, "what *was* that? Placating me? Pretending?"

He can only gape at me for a second.

Finally he says, "If you tell me you don't know that man, then I have to believe you. And you need to believe me about Emily. For some reason, they're trying to drive a wedge between us. If you'll only calm down a second, I'll explain."

"You're the one driving the wedge, Benicio," I say. I snatch my raincoat off the back of the door and head out into the front room.

Isak jumps to his feet and asks where I'm going. He glances around at the others as I slip into my Wellingtons. "Where is she *going*?"

"You know exactly where I'm going," I say. "If you want me to stay you'll need to arrest me."

Meanwhile, Oliver's on the floor hurriedly dumping clothes and books and what all from his own backpack, then thrusting a few things back in.

Moreau enters from the dining room, flaps his phone closed, pockets it. "It was Madame Moreau. Just checking in," he says, as if this is of interest to us all.

"Celia, please," Benicio says. "Really, this...You can't just run off like this."

I hold up my palm. "Watch me," I say.

"Ms. Hagen." Isak steps forward. "We don't want to have to search for you as well."

"I'm capable of taking care of myself," I say. "You might want to review your notes about me and my past."

Isak seems at a loss. Surely he knows I killed a man with a bullet to the throat, knows I ripped open the cut in Jonathon's face with my fingers, yanked his flesh like wallpaper down a wall.

He tries once more to tell me I'll *complicate matters*, that talking to outsiders about the case could be disastrous.

"So much time has been wasted," I say.

He sighs, rubs a hand over his sandy buzz cut, clearly sick of trying to figure out how to deal with me.

I say, "Think of what can happen to an abducted eight-year-old in five days. You *know*?"

I hear Oliver's backpack slump to the floor.

Everyone else has frozen.

Or happened in the first hours...No, I can't say it aloud.

Pinto breaks the silence with a twitchy whine, jumps up and paws at my thigh. "Goddamn it. *Off*," I say.

I never talk to *her* like this either.

"This whole time," I go on, "you led me to believe it's *ransom* they're after—since I have money. Now, who knows *what* you think—that I did it myself, me and some *boyfriend*?"

Isak tries to restore his Interpol face. "Ms. Hagen," he says, "we know this was no spur-of-the-moment thing. It was well planned. You could even say brilliantly. There was inside knowledge, and the execution…the precise cutting of the wires, forcing the stop at just the right place. I admit it has all the makings of a ransom case, but…"

Here Moreau puts out a hand toward Isak's chest, an unsubtle gesture meant to shush him.

After an incredulous moment, Isak defers, turns, and walks off in the direction of the kitchen.

Moreau patiently unwraps a stick of gum and deposits it in his mouth.

"I've been trying to believe you're right, you know," I yell after Isak. "I *needed* to believe it because if he's their ticket to my money, they'll take care of him."

Isak stops, looks back across the room at me. "And why wouldn't this be the case now?"

"Because *clearly* you're fixated on Benicio and me."

"As I've said, this is standard procedure."

"Then use your standard procedure to find out who doctored my phone records," I say.

"Celia," Benicio says. "Take off your jacket." He knows enough not to try to help me out of it. "Maybe you *should* go back," he goes on, "but we need to talk first. You need to understand about Emily."

I realize I cannot bear the sound of his voice another instant. I feel it curdling something in me, turning me sick with loathing. All at once, I'm lunging at him, pummeling his chest. He takes it for a second as if indulging me, a *woman*, but when I swing for his face, he seizes both my wrists.

Left with no other weapon, I plow my knee into his groin.

He jackknifes at the waist, releasing me.

I watch all this as if from above, the pulverizing of my once wonderful life. Then, out of the chaos of shouts and Pinto's yipping and dancing underfoot, Oliver's voice hauls me back, his grip on my upper arms tight enough to bruise. After a moment, I let my muscles go slack. He drops his hands, and we stare at each other. Oh, please don't *you* think I'm a madwoman, I pray silently.

A hand over his heart, Benicio coughs, catches his breath, shakes his head in a way that says, *I no longer have a clue who we are.*

I see Isak's horror, and the looks on the faces of the others crowding around now, men I don't even know, invading my home, my life, their thoughts palpable. *Violent. Unpredictable. Watch her.*

"You all can hang around here waiting for the brilliant kidnapper to let you know how much he wants for my son. Tell your jokes, eat your little boxes of takeout, twiddle your thumbs."

Oliver swipes the copied notes off the dining room table into his backpack, which he zips and throws over his shoulder.

I open the door. "If you all were a little more brilliant yourselves you'd see that Isabel or Jonathon is behind this. And don't stand there and tell me they're in prison, for god's sake."

"Let's go," Oliver says.

"Oliver—" Benicio says.

"It's nothing personal," Oliver says. "It's just, what if she's right?"

We slip out into the breezeway. Before the door shuts, I glance back and see Moreau casually chewing his gum, smiling at me. "I, for one, have indeed read up on you," he says, and hands me a card from his pocket. "I suppose I'll see you back in Saint-Corbenay."

I drop the card in my purse.

And then he winks at me; the cheekiness stops me in my tracks. *Atta girl*, he seems to be saying. *You're on the money now.*

PART TWO

CHAPTER NINE

Saturday morning in summer means riding our bikes to the farmer's market, where I pick up sunflowers for the kitchen and dining room, and Benny plucks through leafy greens, berries, herbs, smoked meats, and cheeses. We pile it all into our panniers and ride the heavy, lopsided bicycles home. Over a month ago, Benny bought *Johannisbeeren* and made a sweet and savory syrup for pancakes. He lined ten small glass bottles on the kitchen counter and asked me to help fill them. "It looks like we're bottling blood," I said of the bright red liquid.

A moment later, strangely, Benny asked what a bloodline was.

"A bloodline? Where'd you hear that word?"

"I don't know," he said, eyeing the neck of the bottle.

"Well, why do you ask?"

"Is it a bad word?"

"No, no. I'm just curious."

He seemed to be only half-listening, the rest of him lost to the chemistry of food.

"I think it's mainly used with animals," I said. "Like dogs? Breeders might want their dogs to have longer noses or a better coat, that kind of thing. They can even breed for how good a dog is at sniffing out rabbits or being around kids. That make sense?" I was hoping I didn't have to get into the actual *breeding* part.

But Benny said, "Like hybrid tomatoes?"

I laughed. "Exactly. Like hybrid tomatoes."

He gave away his syrup to the vendors, the ones who always grin and holler "*Grüetzi*" when they see him coming, who ask how his basil cream chicken or chocolate mousse turned out, or whether the trumpet mushrooms worked in place of the chanterelles. Some of them sell their wares at the Christmas market, and last year Benny baked them cinnamon stars, also jam and butter cookies. He's always seemed more comfortable with adults than with children.

Still, *bloodline*. Where *had* he picked that up?

We cross the border at Basel, and as I drive on toward Saint-Corbenay with Oliver asleep beside me, I have plenty of time to think. I remember how those vendors told me, as people frequently do, how lucky I am to have such a child. Then I'm usually asked (even more often than I'm asked the dreaded writer question, *Where do you get your ideas?*): "So do Benny's talents come from you or your husband?" I always answer: "Benny is one of a kind." Benny's response is always the same too. He takes hold of my hand and smiles, as if to say it doesn't matter. But there is also an air of concern in that smile, as if he's trying to protect me from the truth.

I drive the Range Rover as far as Dijon and stop for the night. Oliver staggers through a fog of jet lag into his room next to mine. By the time my head hits the pillow, I understand that something integral is cracking within me. Sorrow and grief and fear are mounding a suffocating weight on me, but it's not only that—I feel as though a part of my spirit has gone dead, and the rest becoming hard, calculating.

In my sleep, I see Benny sprawled across train tracks, surrounded by strangers. A man draws a blanket over his tiny body. I can't reach him fast enough, can't stop his face from being covered. *Move back, move back*, I scream, but no one understands. I fly into a rage—yank hair, bloody noses, knock teeth from lips that say nothing.

I jolt upright and thump my hand across the bed beside me. Benny is gone. So is Benicio. My knuckles throb from where I must've whacked them on the carved headboard. I gather the duvet to my throat. It smells of bleach, and this brings with it the memory of comfort and order, of mothering, and of my own mother. Her gentle voice in my head eventually settles my breathing.

All night, in the near distance, cars rush along the Autoroute. A small child could be tucked into any of those backseats. Or rope-bound in the back of any truck or van. He could be in Africa, he could be down the hall. The world is too vast. How I crave just a single nugget of a solid fact.

I swing my feet to the floor, throw open the drapes to a violet-black sky, and stare for all the hours it takes for daylight to come and release me.

We breakfast in the hotel restaurant, a long chamber with windows spanning an entire wall. Outside, a strip of morning fog clings to a hillside, making it difficult to see beyond the grassy grounds. The air around us smells of polished wood, fried onions, French coffee; any other morning, we'd leave this table keen on exploring…

Oliver asks if I slept all right.

"I was dead to the world," I say without a qualm.

I wash a generous potato galette down with two cafés au lait, the most I've eaten at a sitting in nearly a week. I pray it doesn't all come back up.

Finally, I say, "Oliver, I hope you know what Moreau said last night about me and the man from the train wasn't true. I've never seen him before in my life."

"Of course I know. But I've been wondering about him, Moreau…did he make all that up, or does he really believe it? I mean, are there actually *texts*?"

"Can you fake something like that?"

"I have no idea, but it doesn't seem impossible."

I nod.

"How well do you know Isabel?" he asks, then glances down at the copied police notes as if not wanting to see my reaction.

"It depends on what you mean by *how well*."

"Has Benicio said what she was like before all the Mexico stuff?"

"A little, not much."

"Tell me the little, then." He looks up with just his eyes.

"She was, *is*, his little sister and I know he was protective of her. He tried to convince her to stay away from Leon and the business with your father. But she wouldn't listen. *Obviously*."

"What about her…as a person?"

What comes to me first is her disdain, how it radiated off her like a toxic aura as she grabbed my hair and stuck the gun barrel to my skull.

"Why are you asking me this?"

"Just making conversation," he answers. A small joke.

And so I give him back a small smile, then he says, "It's just you're so sure she was involved, which seems pretty reasonable, considering."

"Thank you. Apparently, you're the only one who sees it that way. Everyone else thinks I'm totally unbalanced on the subject of Isabel." My face flushes as I remember the scene with Benicio at the door.

Apparently, Oliver remembers too. He glances toward the window. "Do you remember anything else Benicio told you about her? Anything at all, no matter how random?"

"To be honest, she's a topic we stay away from. I mean, he's said general stuff, their having to share everything, for instance, even a bike. It was too big for her, but he said she rode it all around town anyway, standing on the pedals."

"Hmm."

"Not very illuminating."

His shrug says, *It's OK, we'll figure it out.*

"I know a part of him was destroyed by how things turned out in Mexico. I'm making some assumptions here, obviously, but she's his only sibling. They were close growing up—after their parents died, he was her father figure."

I can't forget the look that passed between the two of them after she'd belted me in the face and he'd leapt to my defense, slamming her to the floor. You could see their shock, as both remembered who they'd been to each other, their entwined histories, then the awareness that the bond had just vanished, irretrievably.

Oliver taps his pen on the table and gazes out the windows.

"What are you thinking?" I ask.

"You have every right to hate her, Mom. But I'm wondering… I mean, do you think she was a good mother to Benny? Before everything happened?"

"Oliver, please."

"I know this sounds messed up, but don't you wonder whether what she did back then was for Benny's sake?"

"She tried to kill me, Oliver."

He touches my hand. "It's unforgivable. I'm not excusing anything. I just wonder what her motivation was from the start. Mostly, I guess, I'm wondering how much influence Dad had over her."

"Well," I say, my blood beginning to cool. "I suppose you're right to ask. In fact, it's why her sentence was shorter than it should've been for attempted murder. Her lawyer proved your father had *undue influence* over her."

The mention of his father seems to kill our desire to go on talking. We finish our coffee to the sounds of tableware being cleared away.

Before we get back in the Rover and onto the Autoroute, I withdraw ten thousand euros in cash from my bank's branch in Dijon. If Interpol or anyone else is following me, I won't make it easier by leaving a credit card trail.

It's late morning, and we're just outside of Saint-Corbenay. The sky expands like the swath of a paintbrush, periwinkle, so deep it sends a purplish hue onto the silvery bark of plane trees. The place seems enchanted, as if a warm sedative were infused into the air.

My phone rings between the seats. Benicio has called repeatedly between last night and this morning. Each time, Oliver eyes the buzzing phone, then me. Again, I ignore it, and again I silently refuse to engage Oliver in conversation about Benicio.

Half a year, I think, Benicio and Emily were texting—or longer if he's fudging that too. There's no way they didn't see each other in LA.

No one is above *anything* if the circumstances are ripe. I know this, of course—I know it but let myself forget. I'm my own best example. I've done atrocious things to other human beings when I had to. Likewise, atrocious things have been done to me. I can't escape the fact that they happened, in part, because I'd stopped paying attention to my life. I'd been turning a deaf ear to Jonathon's lies for years by the time all hell broke loose. And now, for all I know, this same complacency was the essential ingredient in Benny's abduction.

The phone stops ringing. A moment later, it starts again.

Oliver sighs, deep and loud. "What if it's about Benny?"

"I'll know," I tell him. "Trust me."

Oliver shakes his head, as if to say, *Isn't that wishful thinking?*

Twenty minutes later a light rain has returned and the hypnotic thump of wipers replaces the ringing phone. Outside, vineyards, valleys, hardwoods soaked to the roots. Another castle looking haunted in the rain.

"Have I been a bad mother?" I ask.

"The worst."

"Oliver—"

"Of course not. Don't talk like that."

"I feel like I've never been able to give enough attention to either one of you. I never made you my *everything*, the way other mothers seem to do. I've always had…other goals, my work—"

"That's sounding pretty retro," he says.

"It's a struggle, believe me. Each part of you wants the upper hand, and you end up feeling like you're lousy at both. Especially when things go to shit. Pardon my French."

Oliver gives me this beautifully adult smile, and says, "Mom, listen to me. Benny knows how much you love him. He *knows*. It's just not an issue."

A sudden convulsion of tears grips me. I cup my mouth, and the feeling disappears surprisingly quickly.

"You're a *great* mother," Oliver says, touching my arm. "And I'm not just saying that. You should hear the stories I've heard from friends about *their* mothers. No, you shouldn't. It's depressing. Seriously. Don't be hard on yourself. I know what you're thinking. Benny's disappearance isn't your fault."

If only this were true.

Oliver scratches his two-day stubble. "Benny's a great kid. And I'm not so bad myself. Well, these days. And we didn't get this way by accident."

I pat his knee. "Thank you."

Part of me believes him—out of a fierce need for it to be true. But the spritz of relief I feel wears off in moments, as I face the possibility that I've been a bad partner to Benicio. How can I not have seen there was trouble in our marriage? Why would Benicio see Emily behind my back unless she was meeting a need of his I somehow wasn't?

Diverting to such thoughts when my concentration should be zeroed in on Benny is just more proof of my failure as a mother. But, even worse, every time I get sidetracked, if only momentarily, the reality of Benny's situation swings back and smacks me anew. It's as if he's being taken from me hundreds of times a day.

"I mean it, Mom."

"All right," I say. "Thank you."

"*Nichts zu Danken*," he says.

The GPS directs us to the train stop at the edge of town. And, suddenly, there's the concrete platform, the Saint-Corbenay sign. I've tried to prep myself, but my stomach clenches at the sight regardless.

I rise from the Rover and suck in a breath. A faint, misty rain glazes my face and hair. I cinch the belt of my raincoat. My steely resolve remains in place.

Oliver covers his head with his hood.

"Do you have some kind of hat?" I ask.

"No. Why?"

"You look too American. Here. Share my umbrella. I don't want us to stand out."

Oliver tosses his hood back and ducks beneath the umbrella. He pulls up a map of Saint-Corbenay on his phone and tugs the image around with his finger. I repeatedly poke him in the head with the umbrella as we set off down a street whose cobalt sign nailed to a stone house reads "Rue de Saint-Corbenay."

"And speak German to me," I say.

"*Klar doch*," he says.

At first, we see no one. Hear no one. The village appears as abandoned as it did last week. The narrow walkways between houses and shops are murky, the cool cobbles slick with age, steaming from warm rain. I've lived in Europe seven years and I'm used to the old world appearance of things, but the handmade lace curtains in the windows, the absence of cars, the silence, leave me feeling as if I've journeyed back centuries.

But then, we hear a soft warble of voices, then the clang of a bicycle bell, then a church bell chiming eleven times. We turn a corner and the rumble of a hundred conversations billows toward us. Oliver locates us on the map, says, "Ah, the town square is a block this way."

We round a corner and come face-to-face with an open-air market, the gurgling fountain in the center of the square. A woman hails shoppers to her jars of mustard. People mill about beneath yellow-and-white-striped awnings between rows of produce—greens, white cabbage, bundled carrots, shallots, a vibrant, autumn-colored display of jams. The rich, fermented smell of cheese reaches my nose, and then I see the stall filled with balls of white and yellow, foamy squares, triangles of marbled blue. Next to that, tables with wicker baskets full of cured meats, sausages the shape and size of yams. And then, arrays of spices, basket after basket.

I could never have imagined this scene when I leaned my head out of the train last week—Saint-Corbenay had seemed so somber and humorless, but of course, I wouldn't have seen it as anything other than forbidding as I searched for Benny.

Now I can't help thinking that this market would be heaven for him. He'd want to dip his nose into every last thing, sniff and fondle, beg for vegetables and bulk spices. His version of a candy shop. My throat tightens at the thought.

I take another long, damp breath, and look around. "I don't see a lot of children," I say.

Oliver clicks pictures with his phone, slowly, in a circle, recording the panorama. "Most kids aren't like Benny," he says. "They don't get excited about going to the market with *Maman*." He lowers the phone and throws me a tight-lipped smile.

"I suppose."

Still, the absence of children seems odd.

"Besides that," Oliver says, "the birthrate has been falling across Europe for decades. These villages are dying. Huge issue for pensioners."

"This village doesn't look like it's dying, Oliver."

"Well, maybe not this one. I've been thinking about that British woman, the witness on the train? I read in *The Times* how Brits are throwing money at ruined farmhouses down here, turning them into B&Bs. It's actually *saving* some of these villages. Maybe that's happening here."

"Hmm," I say. "Moreau was telling me the same thing." I think of the Roma, or Gypsies, as they're called, and of the stranger who spoke to Moreau's daughter, who may have been the man from the train. According to Moreau, he spoke French with some kind of accent. I wouldn't have known the difference.

I draw in the umbrella as we duck and stroll beneath the awnings. I can feel Benny's presence in the shades of green and orange, in the smell of soil and roots, the sharp ripening of fruit. I stop in front of a mound of chervil. The cool strings weave through my fingers as I bring them to my nose. It smells like Benny. It may as well be his clothes, his blanket, his hair between my fingers.

Oliver rubs my back. I press my bottom lip between my teeth.

"We'll find him, Mom," he whispers in my ear. "We will."

I release the chervil, and we walk on. I picture Moreau here, sauntering between the vintners, farmers, housewives, neighbors he'd know by name. Has he *questioned* any of them—despite Interpol's desire to keep the disappearance under wraps? If not, how could he possibly go about the search?

We pass a palette of freshly cut flowers—reds the color of Tabasco, pale yellows, blues, midnight to icy. I think of the unapologetic Madame Moreau—is she one of the women with string bags and gray raincoats, hair pinned at the nape of their necks? No one seems colorful enough. No one shines. I picture her painting nudes into cliffs. I see the love so clearly in Moreau's eyes when he speaks of her, and without warning, I think of Benicio, his lazy finger skimming the base of my throat, drifting along the tender skin behind my ear where his hand cups my head, draws me to his kiss. He calls me "hot fondue." I say, "That's molten cheese to you," and we laugh against each other's teeth.

I lower myself to a bench in the open square. My body feels small and adrift, like a doll tossed out to sea. I cover my head with the umbrella.

"*Alles in ordnung?*" Oliver asks.

"I'm fine, sweetheart," I say softly.

"So?"

"Nothing."

He nods.

I nod back, then give a tiny head tilt toward the crowd. "Why don't you go take more pictures. Scout around."

"Should I pretend to be Swiss?" he asks.

"You *are* Swiss."

"You know what I mean."

"Yes."

So Oliver sets off bareheaded along the perimeter of the market. His hair immediately frizzes. He's tall, his jacket red, easy to spot in a crowd.

I dial Benicio's cell.

He answers with a growling burst of air. "Please tell me you're coming home," he says.

"We just got here," I say.

For a moment, there's nothing but the mustard woman yelling, "*Moutarde!*"

"I'm going out of my mind without you," he says.

"I just want to know if there's any news."

"Celia."

"*Answer* me."

"No. No news."

I let it sink in. Could he be lying? But why would he?

"The last thing we needed was a distraction like this," I say. "This Emily thing."

"No kidding."

I can't help but laugh. "You act like it wasn't your doing."

"It's complicated, Celia. I wanted to talk face-to-face, but you were being so—"

"Why don't you just tell me you slept with her, and get it over with?"

"Because I *didn't* sleep with her. I didn't *begin* to sleep with her."

"I don't believe you."

"You have no reason not to."

"Ha! How many times did you see her in LA?"

"*Moutarde délicieuse!*" the woman yells.

"Never mind," I say. "I don't want to know."

But he goes on anyway, "A producer's interested in one of my scripts, and he wanted to see if Emily was good for a part. OK? It wasn't my idea—I had *nothing* to do with setting it up."

"So, what, you met her at his office?"

"It was a party, actually."

"How nice," I say. "For you both."

A ridiculously long silence follows.

"You have to come home," he says at last.

"You've been texting each other for months, Benicio. How could you not tell me? This isn't like you. Or maybe it *is*. What do I know? You obviously had some reason for doing it on the sly."

"It wasn't to hurt you," he says. "I didn't want to involve you, that's all. You've been busy with the book—"

"I know your voice, Benicio. There's more you're not telling me. You're a bad liar."

"I wish you wouldn't do this."

Me, I think.

"You know what, Benicio," I say after a few moments. "When I do come back, I'm pretty sure I don't want you to be there."

"This is nuts. We obviously can't do this over the phone. I'd come and get you, but I can't leave. In case—"

"I shouldn't have called," I say. "I should've known better."

"Goddamn it, Celia. OK, look, maybe I can—"

"You're *not* coming here. And I'm not coming back without Benny."

He doesn't respond for a while. Then he says, "Just remember what Isak said. If you start asking questions, everyone's going to know the whole story. He could be right, you know, Isak. You could be making things way worse."

It occurs to me that Isak is probably listening in—why didn't I realize that earlier? Benicio could very well be playing along.

I shake my head. This call has exhausted me. I consider just hanging up.

Then, across the way, an old woman catches my eye as she stows leeks and cabbage in her bike basket. Her stockings sag at the ankles. The laces in her black leather shoes are much too long, leaving stringy, oversize loops dragging on the ground. She turns, and unexpectedly smiles at me. If my mother were still alive, she'd be about her age. My mother would have loved it here. Loved my home in Zurich. Loved Benicio, in fact, and so I cannot help but smile strangely, achingly, at this woman as she hops on her bike with tremendous grace and raises her hand into a wave but never looks back. I have the urge to follow wherever she's going.

Benicio says, "Isak told us it could be at least a week before we heard something. It hasn't been quite that long."

"Benicio—" I say.

But a hand suddenly jerks my arm from behind, and the phone leaps from my grasp, tumbles through the air, and smashes against the hard cobblestone.

"*Scheisse!* " I yell.

"You need to come, fast," Oliver says, cupping my elbow, pulling me to my feet.

His stiff, damp face resembles beeswax.

I leap off the bench and snatch up the phone before Oliver pulls me away. Wet slivers of glass crumble in my palm. "*Was ist los?*"

I'm scrambling to keep pace with Oliver's long legs, running while trying to appear as if I'm not. "You're drawing *attention* to us," I hiss in English. "Slow down. Tell me what's going on."

"There's something you need to see," he says, his face growing paler still.

CHAPTER TEN

When I was ten, my parents took me to the Rose Festival along Portland's waterfront. They weren't big on fairs—in fact, we'd never been. I could see my father's patience wearing after walking around in the rain, forking out dimes for games he couldn't win, picking cotton candy out of my hair, enduring an endless Ferris wheel ride with me while the wind shook our rickety metal cage. But leaving the grounds, his face grew fascinated as we stopped to watch a man sketching charcoal portraits. The Rat Pack was displayed behind him—Dean Martin, Sammy Davis Jr., Frank Sinatra, along with Marilyn Monroe, Tom Selleck, and Don Johnson. But it was the one the man was sketching right then that impressed my father. The likeness of the moon-faced woman, streaks of gray at her temples, posing stiff-backed in the chair, was uncanny. More than that, something deeper shone through. Her nature? Except, maybe a *better* her—at least that's what my mother said when they decided to have the man draw me.

Not only did the portrait look like me, but he'd sketched my hair slightly longer than it was, making it the length I was dying for it to reach. My folks hung it in the front hallway—it was the first thing you saw walking in. Within a few months, my hair had caught up with the girl's in the picture; even my eyes had matured into hers. This is what I remember as Oliver pulls me beneath the awning, where a man's sketching a woman of seventy or so in a floppy blue chapeau. But then I think, *Oliver's never seen the picture from the Rose Festival, what's he trying to tell me?*

Instead of the Rat Pack, French celebrities adorn the easels behind him. I recognize Catherine Deneuve, a Roman fountain spraying behind her swooped-up hair. Others, with the French tricolor waving in the background, I take to be politicians. Each sketch is protected by a clear plastic sleeve.

I've dropped the broken phone into my pocket but am still trying to brush the glass from my hand.

The artist jokes with his subject, makes her laugh, then seems to tell her with a shake of his head and finger, *Non*, she must stop laughing, which makes her laugh all the more. Meanwhile, I study the sketches behind him, then turn to Oliver, and mouth, "*What?*"

He throws a quick look over his shoulder to see if anyone's paying attention to us, then guides me to one side of the barrel-shaped friend or sister of the woman being sketched, who's been blocking my view. Now I see a series of children's portraits on small easels—one appears to be three siblings, their heads arranged in a triangle. Beautiful children with large black irises and wavy hair.

"So there *are* kids," I whisper in German.

He shakes his head no.

No, *what*?

I hear Oliver's phone buzzing in his jacket pocket, see the screen glowing through the fabric.

He ignores it.

I follow his line of sight once again until I finally see what's excited him.

A stack of portraits lies on the ground beneath the easels. The one on top is of a young boy. It's *Benny.*

I dig my nails into Oliver's arm, embedding glass slivers in the fleshy part of my fingers, leaving little jots of blood on the sleeve of his hoodie.

He turns us away from the crowd.

"Where the hell did it come from?" I whisper.

Leaning in, he says, "I'm going to ask if it's for sale. Play it cool."

"What if he's the man who *took* him?" I say through my teeth. Instantly, I realize how idiotic this is, and shoot Oliver a look, *Sorry, it's my paranoia talking.* But then I say, "Oh, what if it's *not* him?"

"*Mom.*"

"Just a boy who looks like him?"

"In this tiny town. What are the chances?"

"What should we do?"

The phone buzzes again in his pocket.

"Here, give me that."

Oliver hands it over, forces a smile, pivots, nonchalants his way into the booth, and watches the man work, even chuckles at his jokes (which, of course, he doesn't understand).

"*Excusez-moi,*" Oliver finally says.

"Yes?"

"Oh. You speak English."

"Indeed, I do," the man says. "Would you like a portrait?"

Oliver looks at me. So much for speaking German.

The old woman in the chair and her companion drop their smiles and stare at my son.

"Actually, I was wondering about some of those behind you," Oliver says.

"You're a fan of Chirac?"

"It's just so well done."

"*Merci.*"

"Are those for sale as well?" Oliver points to the portraits of children.

"*Oui.* If you like. I draw also from photographs. The children cannot sit so well as…" He nods at the woman in the chair.

"May I look through them?" he asks, pointing.

"*Mais oui.*" The man lifts the whole pile onto the table for him. "You like these, the children?"

"I'm a teacher," Oliver says. "They'd look great in my classroom back in the States. It's nice for our kids to see others from around the world."

I'm struck again by the competent liars in my family.

"Please," the man says. "Take your time."

As he wipes his hands on an already blackened towel, I get my first good look at them, the black-rimmed nails. A shot of dread whooshes through me: Helena Watson, the British witness, had described the stranger's fingernails as chewed or chipped, with dark stains beneath them.

The artist meets my eyes and nods hello. "A portrait for madame?" His hair is dusky black, straight and in need of a trim. A fine white scar shows through the charcoal stubble on his chin, the kind one gets from falling against a table edge as a child. He must be in his late fifties. He looks nothing like the man on the train.

"No," I say. "Thank you. *Merci.*"

The two old women turn to look at me like dogs sniffing the air. I slip my bloody hand into my pocket as they fidget, agitated by all the interruption.

"How about this one?" Oliver holds up the portrait of Benny, and there's no question that it's him. The streaks in his hair, the immense lashes. Down to the shape of his teeth. In fact, the pose, the cant of his head—a gesture so familiar to me I can't bear to look at it.

Oliver lowers the portrait to the pile with a shaky hand. I pretend interest in the next table's steamy smell of egg, crepes sizzling on a hot metal drum.

I don't know if it's the smart thing to do. Maybe seeing Benny's face has softened me, or my nerves have made me desperate—whichever, I text Benicio from Oliver's phone. *It's Celia. My phone broke.* I get the feeling he might need to know this at some point for reasons I can't yet imagine.

"Lovely. Lovely boy, no?" I hear the artist say.

"Is he a relative?"

"*Non.*"

Oliver nods. I will him to be careful, not ask too many questions.

"On my way to the market, I see this photograph on the ground," the artist says, looking only at his subject, his charcoal sweeping across the thick paper. "Beautiful child. Full, beautiful life. You see in the eyes."

Oliver nods, a terrible strain in his face.

A vague connection to something, a memory, is tugging at me; a sense of déjà vu rushes in, and then out.

The woman in the chair adjusts her hat, and the man lowers his arms and mock chides her again about sitting still. She laughs and slides her hands beneath her thighs.

"Too bad you don't know him. It's always nice to have a story to tell the children," Oliver says.

"Perhaps a tourist dropped the photograph from a bag. You could tell the children a story about this."

Oliver nods at the portrait. "Is it recent?"

"*Oui*. About two weeks? *Oui*, I think two, maybe three weeks."

Weeks! How can this be? Clearly we're both thinking the same thing. Benny was taken six days ago. How did the photo show up here *two weeks* ago?

"How about I take these three on top?" Oliver says calmly. "The two boys and the girl?"

"No Chirac for you today?"

"Sure. I'll take Chirac, as well," Oliver says with his single-dimpled smile. "*Vive la France.*"

The man grins as he wraps the plastic-covered sketches in butcher paper and ties them with twine. He hands the package to Oliver in exchange for the euros.

I feel as if I'm about to burst. We can't just walk away without the photograph.

The line of people waiting for crepes now stretches into the square. Everyone seems to know one another, chatting forward and behind. A young girl with wavy red hair holds her small blue umbrella in one hand, the edge of her mother's jacket pocket in the other. I have the urge to rush over and make sure they know how lucky they are to be sharing a crepe in the rain.

I feel the mother's eyes on me. She has caught me staring at her child. I turn and pretend to talk on Oliver's phone.

Then, just as Oliver is about to walk away, I hear him say, "I'm curious, if you don't mind. I'd love to see the likeness you drew from. You wouldn't happen to have the original photos of the children, would you?"

The women turn and study him. What kind of person asks such questions? The artist himself looks wary. "I find the process fascinating," Oliver goes on. "How you manage to transfer every bit of light and nuance from one medium to the next."

Does the artist understand him? He seems to at least get the gist and takes it as a compliment. He reaches into what looks like a tackle box full of charcoal crayons, pencils, and a money pouch. He lifts up one of the trays and retrieves several photographs, which he hands to Oliver.

It's all I can do to hang back and appear disinterested.

Oliver nods as he shuffles through the photos. "You're very talented," he says. "Are you a teacher as well?"

The old women have had just about enough. They look at their wristwatches and sigh.

"*Non. Merci*!" the man says. "I do it only for me. There's no time for teaching. I have a vineyard as well."

"Ah! A dream of mine," Oliver says. "How wonderful."

I slide up next to him.

The artist says something to the woman, though she seems reluctant to laugh. "*Voila*!" he says, spinning the easel around for her to see.

The women flutter and cry out; at the same instant, Oliver slips the photo of Benny into the twine underneath the portraits in his hand. He places the rest on the table.

"*Merci beaucoup*, and *au revoir*," he says and practically pushes me toward the line for crepes.

"*Merci*!" the man calls out with a wave of his hand, his attention returned to the women.

We cross the square and duck into a narrow walkway. Oliver holds the umbrella above our heads. I exchange his phone for the photograph.

Benny. Oh god. It's truly him. The vague tugging in the back of my mind suddenly pops free. "I shot this photo *myself*, no more than a month ago at Confiserie Sprüngli, our favorite confectionery in Zurich. Then I framed and hung it with the family portraits in the living room."

CHAPTER ELEVEN

It's as if something putrid has been shoved beneath my nose. I bend over and grip my knees. I imagine a set of hands I must know, eyes I should recognize, peering through the rooms of my house, my *home*, once filled with *Liebe und Glück*. Footsteps, a voice, whispering to Benny. Someone we trust. Someone we love. *Who* took this photograph from my wall?

I bend the photo into my pocket, cover my mouth, and lurch away from Oliver. I retch beneath the golden-stained windows of a brasserie; its red velvet drapes blocking the patrons from the spattering potato galette. My throat burns. The blood behind my eyes pulses and pushes as if urging me to see the very thing I don't want to look at.

I need to talk to Benicio.

Oliver rests his hand on my shoulder. Covers me from the rain.

"Can you hand me a tissue from my purse?"

Oliver digs out several, holds them in the rain, and then hands me the damp lump.

"Thank you." I wipe my mouth, spit flecks of galette from my teeth. "I need some water, sweetheart."

"I don't want to leave you here."

"I'm all right."

But I'm not. I'm shaking. I step away from the windows and rest my back to the stone wall. "The picture was in a frame on our living room wall."

Oliver leans beside me, mouth gaping.

"I don't *believe* this," I say. "Whoever took him must have been in our *house*, Oliver. It makes my skin crawl. Someone I may have offered food, wine, stories, including ones about Benny."

"There's got to be an explanation," Oliver says.

The phone buzzes in his pocket.

I spit again.

"I saw some Perrier at the cheese stand," Oliver says.

"Yes, go," I say, then nod at his pocket. "That's probably Benicio. Don't tell him about the photograph. Don't tell *anyone*."

"Isak?"

"I'm pretty sure he thinks I'm behind the whole thing, if he can just figure it out. I can't imagine what he'll make of the photo being here ahead of Benny missing. More trickery on my part, I guess. But the last thing I want is to give him another reason to arrest me."

Oliver eyes me steadily, deciding whether or not to obey me. I almost can't bear the power of this gaze. "All right," he says finally, returns the umbrella, and puts on his hood. "Wait here."

The photograph looks stepped on, smudged with charcoal dust—useless as a source of fingerprints at this point, no doubt. There on the back in my own hand: *Benny, 7 years old, Zurich. 03 Juni, 2009.* And a tiny smear of blood from where I first touched it a few minutes ago.

I'm sure I had it framed and on the wall within a week—by the tenth, then. And if it's been here roughly two weeks, that would make it sometime in the last month and a half or so that it was taken. Who was at the house during that time?

I pull out my phone to check the calendar, forgetting it's broken.

Scheisse.

But my laptop is in the Rover, synched with the phone.

"Here you go," Oliver says, opening the bottle of Perrier, putting it into my hand.

"Thank you." Even the lukewarm bubbles sting my raw throat. After drinking as much as I can stand, I ask, "Do you remember me mentioning any guests? Sometime within the last month?"

"Sorry, no," Oliver says.

I sag a little. "My short-term memory is shot," I say. "I'm not thinking straight."

"Benicio might remember something."

"*No*," I say, too sharply. "I said I don't want him to know what we found."

"I get that."

"I'm not sure you do."

"I get the gist of it, Mom. And considering the questions Moreau was asking me…are you two *all right*? I mean, before all this?"

"I don't know."

I see Oliver cringe. I feel so sorry for him. "Look, sweetie," I say, "we have to stay focused on Benny, OK?"

"Right."

I say, "Whoever stole the photo could've been in the house when I wasn't—he could've been there to see Benicio." *Or she,* I think. *Could've been a she. Emily? No, that's crazy. Some other woman?* A few days ago, I'd have thought that was equally crazy. I try to remember if I was gone any length of time in the last month. Then again, how long does it take to rearrange a few pictures?

"Claudia and Renata cleaned several times, but they're family, and we've used them for years without any problems."

Just then, a man comes hurrying along lugging a cloth satchel bulging from the market, arm pumping at his side. He startles at the sight of us. His face is largely obscured beneath his wool cap, yet it seems to linger on me, then the vomit on the ground. His step slows, then speeds up again.

What must we look like? Strangers in the narrow walkway, the foul spatter on the cobbles, our red, panic-stricken eyes.

We don't say a word until the flare of his trench coat is long gone.

"Did that guy give you the creeps?" Oliver asks.

"Why?"

"I don't know. I guess I'm suspicious of everyone," he says.

"I understand," I say.

Oliver narrows his eyes in the direction the man fled. He pulls up a map of the area on his phone. "Let's go back to the train stop and look around. Or let me look. You can wait in the car and catch your breath."

I slip my hand through the crook of his arm.

Oliver whispers, "I have this feeling Benny's somewhere close. Don't you?"

I look into my son's face and I can barely keep my despair at bay. Even if Benny *is* here, what makes me think I can actually find him? Is this a fool's errand? Have I put us all at risk for nothing?

We reach the Rover, stand aside it, the train platform now directly across an open field. Still a bit nauseous, I'm comforted by the idea of shutting myself up in the front seat and putting my head down. But Oliver wasn't around when Benny disappeared, and won't necessarily know what to look for. The fact is, I need to be on the platform myself.

We set off through wet knee-high grass, flushing out small acrobatic toads. Blackbirds tug at worms until we're practically on top of them. The air smells of wet hay and manure. All's quiet again. It must be some acoustic magic, the layout of the houses and shops, the slope of the hill and short narrow walkways conspiring to carry the sound off into the vineyards.

I climb onto the platform. The fainting woman was here, her husband over there; the others were crouched on either side. I imagine the train on the tracks. Could you sneak a child past this small knot of people? Were they too absorbed in their own problem? What if the child was making a fuss?

And if he wasn't making a fuss, *why not*?

Then it occurs to me to ask Oliver, "The cross-continental trains are *longer* than the locals, aren't they?"

He nods, says they'd have to be.

"So it must've stuck way out," I say, and we both turn and look east, beyond where the platform stops.

Benny could have been at either end of the train, though probably the rear; it would've been simple for them to hop down and cross behind the last car. On the far side of the tracks is a windbreak of twisty-branched plane trees, interspersed with lilac bushes, thick with dried blossoms.

Before coming back here, I thought Saint-Corbenay could have been happenstance, an opportunity presenting itself. After all, how would one calculate how long a train could last with sabotaged air-conditioning before having to stop for repairs? And Saint-Corbenay, tiny, the middle of nowhere? But Benny's photograph being here two weeks ago changes *everything*. I run through what the artist said again, how he seemed. I decide I have to take him at his word.

I study the sky. The rains come in bursts all day, thinning to drizzle, then stopping altogether. Each time I think the storm's blown over, another mass of black roils in. And now, while I'm still looking up, lightning splits the sky. A mix of hail and rain crashes against the umbrella, unbearably loud.

"I want to see what's over there," I tell Oliver when it lets up, nodding toward the other side of the tracks.

The plane trees are set back fifteen or twenty meters from the railbed. Their trunks are thick and mottled, like dots on a paint-by-number set. Side by side, they provide enormous cover. I push through tumbled brush to see a long-neglected vineyard, the brittle, blackened vines in disciplined rows still bound to ancient posts, to wire that has rusted but not given up its grip. Stubborn grapes of all sizes still manage to pop through like a million sweaty blisters. The vineyard backs onto forest, and there's no farmhouse in sight. I walk on a ways to where the rows are interrupted by a bumpy two-track lane, then see, in the soggy ground, a tractor's heavy tread marks.

This brings back the red tractor I mentioned to the hypnotist. It had caught my eye when the train first stopped. It stood alone in the vineyard. I hadn't noticed it again later...but, of course, by then my thoughts were elsewhere. In any case, it's gone today. And what was it doing out here in the first place? The grapes don't seem to have been harvested in decades.

Oliver studies the tracks and then peers at me with a raised eyebrow. I cover my mouth and take in the scent of chervil lingering on my hand. My scalp tingles. Images flash like a premonition, clear and sure. I see Benny propped on the tractor, a laughing driver, a stranger, telling my son *happy birthday*. Telling him *surprise!* Telling him *this is a gift from your parents.*

CHAPTER TWELVE

A distant rumble, then a dazzling beam through the rain, and within moments the brakes on the train hiss as the giant machine halts in front of us. It's slightly longer than the length of the platform. In less than a minute, the driver sounds his horn and we hear metal on metal as the train rolls away. Only one passenger has stepped off. A young man in dark skinny jeans and sneakers lumbers down the platform stairs. He zips his leather jacket and tucks his chin into his collar against the rain. The train is already out of sight. Steam rises and fades from the tracks.

I tell Oliver about the tractor, and in telling him I realize that by the time the man we've been calling the stranger offered to help me, Benny might already have been jouncing away with someone else.

We gaze downhill, where the vineyard appears to curve toward town. Surely Moreau has stood where we're standing now, has seen what we see. Has he come to the same conclusions?

Oliver rubs his eyes and succumbs to a monster yawn.

"Jet lag's eating you alive," I say. "If you need to crash, I understand."

He assures me he's fine, says not to worry, suggests we follow the vineyard down to where it meets the town.

Not so long ago, Oliver couldn't stand the sight of me. Everything I did or said was met with eye rolling and a smart-ass reply—if he replied at all. How he turned out to be one of the kindest people I know, I'll never comprehend. I just wish he were more willing to open up about the past. I can't help believing that what's happened to Benny is at the end of a chain leading back, link by link, to our own particular history. I don't know if it's as simple as Isabel trying to reclaim what she sees as hers, or Jonathon seeking vengeance. Since he'll never spend another day outside prison, revenge would seem to be his *only* motive. But he's a psychopath. I put nothing past him.

Years ago, Jonathon wrote several letters to Oliver. I made a point of leaving them on the kitchen counter, but Oliver tossed each one, unopened, into the recycling bin. I left them there, never knowing what they said. The letters eventually stopped coming. And then, soon after Oliver turned twenty-one, his attitude toward his father began to change. With maturity came curiosity: he wanted to know how Jonathon could've done what he did to us. It's the only time I know of that Oliver visited him.

What went on during that encounter, the emotional chaos Oliver must've endured…this is exactly the kind of thing he's reluctant to share. He's a grown man now. I can't force him to tell me what he'd rather not say. What I *do* know is that Jonathon apologized repeatedly, claimed that years of stress, of compounding each mistake with a worse one, had left him temporarily out of his mind. He claimed it had taken years in prison for him to recover. And now, he said, he was consumed with remorse. I believe none of this, not a word. Finally, after making his case to Oliver, the son of a bitch asked to be forgiven. "And *did* you forgive him?" I've asked Oliver more than once. His answer, each time, has been a single nod, a not-so-convincing yes.

"When we get back to the car, see if you can find us a pension on your phone," I say. "Honestly, you look like you're going to fall over."

He smiles gently from the side of his mouth. "I won't."

So I turn my attention to the ground again, kick the dirt with my boot. Until today's rain, the soil was hard packed from weeks of drought…but before I can follow this thought all the way through, Jonathon interrupts my concentration again. If he's the one who engineered all this, then what has he done with Benny? Who would he give him to? Is it remotely possible that he'd have his own son killed to punish me? I can't let myself believe that… yet this is a man who once threatened to kill Oliver to get me to do his bidding.

My umbrella leans against the tree, its metal tip aimed at the sky. I flip it over and stab it in the ground and tell myself, for god's sake, *focus.*

I ask Oliver, "Could a tractor leave tracks this deep if the soil's so dry?"

"Good question," he answers. "They're pretty heavy, but I'm not sure—"

"Or maybe the tracks are from ATVs," I say. "If the police were searching here. Or vintners going from one field to the other."

I glance east and west. Whatever made the tracks, I have no doubt that the French gendarmes have seen them, not to mention Interpol.

"What do we do now?" I say.

Before Oliver can reply, we hear glass breaking in the distance, followed a split second later by the earsplitting wail of a car alarm.

We cut back through the plane trees and recross the tracks. By the time we reach the platform, the man in the trench coat is fleeing down Rue de Saint-Corbenay with my computer bag clutched to his chest and my backpack swinging awkwardly from one hand.

I'm too stunned to react for a moment, and even after I start to run my legs feel dead—I might as well be running through loose sand. Six days of virtually no sleep, barely any food, my nerves zinging with adrenaline, have left me pathetically frail, at least five kilos lighter. It's all I can do to keep hold of the flopping purse at my shoulder. In seconds, Oliver's way out ahead, a flailing streak of red darting through the flap of blackbirds. The shriek of the alarm manages to pierce the acoustic trickery of the place, traveling around walls, down lanes, drowning out the *moutarde* woman in the village square. For a second, I wonder if Benny hears it too.

Despite the rain, housewives begin poking their heads out second-floor windows. "Shit!" Oliver says, kicking at the nuggets of safety glass. "Shit, shit, shit."

By the time I reach him, I have no breath. The air around my head feels thin, diluted, silvery gray. I can't talk. I cover my eyes. Even a groan takes effort.

Oliver extracts the keys from my jacket pocket. The alarm continues its wail, yet a woman's voice somehow makes itself heard. I drop my hand and see a thin, attractive young woman in jeans and a white blouse approaching from the corner house, where the front door stands open. A cell is clutched in her hand.

"Police," she shouts, the same in English as French. I shake my head no. Wave my hands no. This is the last thing we need.

She chatters on in French as blots of rain darken her blouse, revealing the lace of her bra, and flattening the blonde hair lying across her bony shoulders.

"Police," she shouts again, and then I understand she's already called them.

I doubt Moreau could have returned from Zurich so soon. Anyway, he wouldn't answer a call about a car break-in, would he?

Oliver fumbles with the keypad and manages to kill the alarm. The silence is long, high-pitched, unnerving.

Second-floor windows begin to close.

Oliver opens the rear door, snatches up his backpack and computer bag, shakes the glass free. "He only got yours," he says.

"This is a disaster," I say. "We've got to get out of here. She's called the police."

Oliver appears to notice her only now. She's trying to tell me something else. The rain isn't enough to move her to go inside. She's persistent, shivering, her nipples lifting through the sheer fabric.

I raise my palms and jostle my head. "I'm sorry! I don't speak French!"

"*Sprechen Sie Deutsch?*" she asks, which surprises me more than anything happening here.

"*Ja,*" I tell her, stunned, lowering my hands. Why on earth would she ask me this?

I'm thoroughly soaked, my umbrella abandoned by the plane tree. All of my clothes are in the hands of trench coat man, my hairbrush, toiletries, everything.

The woman glances at Oliver and then the Rover. Of course. The Swiss plate has given us away.

Still, a German-speaking French person in a village this small seems remarkable.

"*Sie sollten beide in das Haus gekommen,*" she says, motioning toward her door.

I glance at Oliver. His hood shadows his forehead, his eyes two dark smudges of fatigue. What is it, three, four o'clock in the morning for him?

He nods and the rain collecting on his hood dribbles down his face. Yes. We should come inside the house.

CHAPTER THIRTEEN

Our host, whose name is Seraphina, hands Oliver a vinyl tablecloth and a roll of duct tape to cover the broken window in the car. I catch him looking at her breasts. How could he not? I can hardly see anything other than the two raised brown dots myself.

I remove my Wellingtons at the door as Oliver goes out.

Seraphina offers me a towel. It smells slightly musty, as if retrieved from a closet that's never opened.

The small front room is steeped in filmy green light thrown from a square stained glass window on the opposite wall. The floor seems an extension of the street outside—large slick stones, wide, smooth grout in between. The kitchen consists of a black-veined porcelain sink, an oven barely as wide as a cake pan, a camper-sized refrigerator, and three feet of freestanding counter. The air smells of cabbage, potatoes, and dust. The dreary orange upholstery, the antennae sprouting from the television…this place looks as it must have long before Seraphina was born. Yet she herself looks every bit a modern Frenchwoman—covetously thin, simply dressed, while somehow throwing off that mythic French self-confidence that reveals itself as style.

I thank her again.

She says she's sorry for my troubles. "*Verbrechen ist im Saint-Corbenay sehr selten*," she says. Crime is very rare in Saint-Corbenay.

"Hmm," I say.

She takes my jacket and invites me to sit at a small kitchen table, her voice a near whisper, as if someone's asleep elsewhere in the house. She goes into a back room and returns moments later wearing jeans and a blue long-sleeved shirt with a scooped neck, her damp hair hastily secured by a Scünci. Her lips look fuller this way. I decide she's likely Oliver's age and childless.

She offers me tea and puts a kettle on the stove, ignites the pilot light with a match. Her fingers are ringless.

She shows me to the bathroom, two narrow doors side by side. One has the bathtub, the other the toilet and sink. I close myself inside the one with the sink.

A small pink crock of what must be cold cream sits on a shelf next to shapely glass jars of blue and pink fluids. A boar-hair brush and hand mirror lie next to it. The brush is lightly strung with gray hair.

Seraphina doesn't live here. *This is not her house.*

The mirror over the sink has lost much of its silvering—a cloudy black river seems to be eating through the glass. I'm barely able to make out my face, but see enough to recognize the gray-blue of my eyes inside mascara-blackened sockets, the dark, wet curls against my bony cheeks.

I rinse beneath my eyes. Water dribbles into my mouth. It tastes like iron. I try to squeeze my hair dry with the towel, then see that my hand has started bleeding again.

I return to the front room, pressing a Kleenex to my hand just as Oliver comes in from outside without knocking. He's clearly shaken, exhausted, cold. He gives Seraphina the duct tape. She smiles, holds a towel out to him, and in her whispery voice offers to take his jacket. He peels it off his body, puddles gathering at his feet. Is getting the floor wet the reason he looks so embarrassed? Or is my normally straight-backed, confident son a little shy with Seraphina's eyes on him? This is a side of him I've never seen. I think of the romance novels I edited years ago, the most depressing episode in my professional life—the coy glances, nervous hands, flushed faces.

Seraphina hangs his jacket near the door. She looks down at my hand.

"*Sie bluten*," she says.

I explain the slivers of broken glass from my phone. She retrieves a set of tweezers, sits across from me with a wet cloth, and carefully cleans out my hand.

The teakettle whistles and Oliver quickly gets to his feet and shuts it off. Seraphina tells him where to find the tea, and he makes three cups and sets ours in front of us. A forced familiarity fills the air.

I can't imagine what's taking the gendarmes so long. The station is at the edge of the village, not far from where we are now. No sooner do I think this than someone knocks. In steps Moreau's subordinate, his thick mustache like a limp mouse glistening around his mouth

He nods a familiar hello to Seraphina. I see from the amount of water on his jacket that he's most likely been right outside, taking note of the Rover. This would explain what's taken so long.

"*Bonjour. Parlez-vous français?*" he asks Oliver.

Oliver shakes his head. "*Sprechen Sie Deutsch?* English?"

The man laughs as if to himself and pulls out a small blue notebook and pen.

"No," he says, and then proceeds to speak English.

"Your name?"

"Oliver Hagen."

Hearing him say his last name reminds me once again that he changed it from Donnelly to Hagen when he turned eighteen.

"Swiss?"

"Yes." Oliver leaves it at that.

"And your name?" the man says.

I assume he means me. His eyes are on his notebook. He continues writing.

"Celia Hagen."

"Swiss?"

"Yes."

Either he's a good actor or his short-term memory is severely impaired.

Seraphina offers him tea.

"*Non. Merci*," he says, all business. He remains in the low-sloped doorway that looks as if it was constructed in the Middle Ages.

"So," he says, suddenly meeting my eyes. "Why are you here, in Saint-Corbenay?" It's as if I'm being accused of a crime.

"Someone broke into my car and stole my computer and backpack," I say. "It had my clothes, toiletries, everything."

He doesn't write this down.

I glance at Oliver. His eyes narrow. "We saw the man," he says. "He was wearing a tan trench coat and wool cap."

The gendarme draws in a breath and says something in French to Seraphina. Apparently, he's reconsidered the tea. Seraphina rises to the stove and pours him a cup.

"We saw him earlier," I add. "Near the market square. He walked by with vegetables in a sack. I'm sure someone in the market will remember him."

The man takes the offered tea, thanks Seraphina, who now busies herself at the sink.

My earlier anger has returned. I want to ask why the hell he's in here drinking tea and refusing to write down what we say. But what I'm *really* angry about is why he's not out looking for Benny.

"What happened to your hand?" he asks.

I don't answer.

He turns to Seraphina and asks her something in French.

Her reply causes him to sneer. "How did the glass get into your hand?" he asks me, and I understand immediately that he thinks I broke into my own car. Oliver opens his mouth but I touch his shoulder.

"I want to speak to Inspector Moreau," I say.

I feel Seraphina spin around at the sink.

Moreau is out of town, the gendarme informs us.

"Then I want to speak to Madame Moreau."

The no longer complacent policeman lowers his mug. He shifts in his wet leather boots, which squeak.

Seraphina comes forward and stares at me with a look of confusion. Apparently, she's understood what I've said.

"*Wie kennen Sie Frau Moreau?*" she asks.

Before I have the chance to tell her how I know of Mrs. Moreau, a thin, scratchy voice calls out to Seraphina from the rear of the house.

"*Moment,*" Seraphina says to me, and heads down the hall.

Oliver eyes me with a look that says he's more than ready to get out of there.

I turn and edge forward in my chair. "Shouldn't you be writing down the information about our car?" I ask the man, who hasn't offered his name, which doesn't appear on the front of his rain jacket either, though I have no doubt he's the same man who sat in the interrogation room while Moreau questioned me last week. Hard to forget a mustache like that. There is no way he could have forgotten me.

Down the hall, the sound of a dresser drawer opens and closes. A door creaks and snaps, a wardrobe, I assume, and then female voices conversing in French.

"You shouldn't be here," the gendarme says.

I swallow my tea and tilt my head to the side. "A thief is running loose in your village. Not to mention a child snatcher. I believe you're the one who shouldn't be hanging around, sipping tea in doorways."

The disdain is palpable through his half grin.

Seraphina is suddenly at the table, her sight volleying between the gendarme's face and mine. The air temperature seems to rise, the scent of dust blooms in the heat.

"Mom," Oliver says.

I set my cup on the table.

"Thank you for your help," I say to the gendarme. "What did you say your name was?"

Just when I'm convinced he won't tell me, he says, "Petit," though his lips barely move.

"Ah. Petit," I say. "Like small. Like undersized." I form a space of two inches between my finger and thumb. "Got it."

CHAPTER FOURTEEN

After buying a few replacement clothes and toiletries in Aix, we return to Saint-Corbenay and rent rooms at a modest pension on the edge of town. Its spareness is a comfort, the simple linens and singular pillow, the disinterested but friendly woman at the reception, a relief.

The first thing Oliver does is check his camera for the panoramic footage he took of the market. He plugs it into his computer and we study each photograph intensely before moving on to the next. Shortly before the final one, we see the silhouette of the trench coat as, apparently, the man converses with the woman selling him what looks like persimmons and melons. In the next one, he's waving good-bye when he leaves as if they're friendly, though it's hard to say with our frustratingly partial view of him. After that, he's gone.

Surely she'd remember him if asked.

"Should we tell Moreau's guy, Petit?" Oliver asks.

"That guy thinks we broke into our own car. Like it's an insurance scam or something. Do they even *have* insurance scams in France?" I rub my eyes. "I can't think straight."

"Me neither," Oliver says. After a moment, he adds, "Tomorrow's Sunday, the market's not open. The next chance we'll have is Wednesday."

"Maybe if we ask around town someone can ID the vendor for us," I say.

"I think I agree with Isak. We can't go asking questions without putting Benny in more danger."

"But we don't know if that's *true*, Oliver. Suppose doing *nothing* is worse."

He frowns, looking as stymied as I feel.

"Let me have your phone," I say.

He fishes it out of his jacket.

I dial Moreau. No answer. "If you need to reach me for anything," I tell his voice mail, "call me back at the number I'm calling on."

I rise, kiss Oliver on the forehead, and go to my room to ready myself for another night of misery.

My own screams wake me. For all my numbness during the day, every cell of me is painfully alert while I sleep. This time I'm not on the train. Neither is Benny. I'm looking through the mottled glass window of a stone house where I see him crouched in a dark corner. He appears to be crying. I bang the glass but he doesn't look up. I run to open the door and someone shoves me against the house, so hard I can't breathe. I catch sight of Benny through the crack in the door. He's pointing and laughing at me. Not crying after all.

I no longer reach for Benicio—that's something. I throw off the woolen blanket, and in the bathroom wipe my neck and forehead with a damp cloth. It's 2:18 a.m., but I'm done sleeping for the night. I settle into a cushioned rattan chair, and look out through the French doors of the balcony. I make myself try to list exactly what's on the stolen computer—family photos from vacations, others taken in the house, plenty of Pinto and Benny playing or sleeping by the fire. One file contains photographs of Benny's dishes, including the ones from the *Food and Wine* magazine article I wrote. What else? Bookmarked links to writerly websites, articles on parenting, and so many other topics that would certainly be useless to a thief. There are links to Oliver's articles as well, but those could just as easily be found doing an Internet search. What was the man hoping to find? My new novel is no longer there, but scraps of notes for other projects are. But who, other than me, could understand what they mean? Are there facts about our private life that appear nowhere else? My financial records? I have no idea. Such a miscellany of files is scattered all over the place that it's impossible for me to reconstruct. I have no idea if my passwords are exposed, popping up automatically when opened. I'm so bad at that sort of thing. What is there, specifically, about *Benny*?

It seems I've broken out in another sweat. After gulping down a cold glass of water, I return to the rattan chair, and am thinking now of Seraphina—young, single, her future wide open in front of her in a way mine will never be again. I remember exactly how that feels—to wake with freedom and discovery surging through my veins, the not knowing what lay ahead fueling the excitement, unlike the fear of the unknown that now renders me somewhat useless, sitting as I am, alone in the middle of the night with no clue of what to do next. And Oliver…it's hard to see him as a man, someone other than my son, my boy, but surely he has that same sense of young independence and possibility. And yet, how different might he be if the tragedy of our past had never happened? I've never stopped worrying about what Jonathon stole from him—not his innocence, which we all lose sooner or later, but the knowledge that there are certain places in the world, certain people, including close loved ones, that Oliver shouldn't have to think twice about trusting without fear, without constant reevaluation.

And Benny? What burden might he carry? What cruelty might never be completely wrung from his spirit? I can't know this—not now, maybe not ever. And I won't make it to morning if I don't let these thoughts rest, so I will my mind back to the sunnier picture of Oliver and Seraphina and their bright futures, and for a while this actually works. I recall how shortly after Monsieur Petit had made his swift exit from Seraphina's house, I felt more protective of Oliver than ever, which somehow translated into me asking Seraphina what she did for a living.

"Nothing yet, really," she said. "I'm still a student. At the University of Berlin."

Oliver asked what she was studying.

German, she told him. "My father was a professor of European history. I want to teach literature."

Oliver looked as though he'd just drawn the lucky ticket. He gave me the eye: *Tell her who you are!* But I was in no mood to say, *Oh, yes, you probably know my novel, it was on the best-seller list for months...* Instead, I asked what had brought her to Saint-Corbenay.

"My aunt. This is hers," Seraphina said, with a tiny wave at our surroundings. "She's my only family, and she hasn't long to live."

"I'm so sorry," I said, and I was. The thought of her alone in the world gave me a pang—I was her age when I lost my mother, the last of *my* family. Or so I'd believed at the time. It would be years before I discovered teams of cousins, aunts, and uncles. Switzerland is a small country that sometimes feels more like a small town. Practically everyone is related in one way or another.

Seraphina nodded thoughtfully.

In the street three floors below my room, a car door closes with a quick, solid thud. Then another. A motor starts, the car speeds off. I open the balcony door and slip into the predawn. The car is already out of sight, leaving behind a quiet filled only by cicadas. A light inside a cooler in the *Imbiss* across the street glows behind posters of ice cream and coffee taped in the windows. The smell of pinewoods blows down from the hills, dry and cool. All of this seems so ordinary, so harmless. Nothing noteworthy in the picture except the nightgowned woman on the balcony, praying for the safe return of her child, for one small clue that could change everything.

I don't think I've ever felt so alone. I barely register the presence of my own body. I remember the gutted feeling in my core when Oliver was on the run from Jonathon. What I feel now is different. For one thing, I knew where Oliver was, I could reach him if I needed to—he was only lost from Jonathon's point of view. And he was much older than Benny. Big enough to put up a fight.

I open my eyes to a sound I don't recognize, a murmur coming from above. Braced against the railing, I look up to see a gigantic flock of small dark birds, starlings by the thousands undulating above my head, so close that the air around me thrums with their power. My nightgown swooshes through my legs from the breeze. I am spellbound as they stream past, shifting shapes like a school of fish swirling in a great, wide ocean.

Benny, Benny, Benny.

CHAPTER FIFTEEN

Without telling me, Oliver heads out early to retrieve Moreau's address from Seraphina. Or so he says. I don't even know he's gone until he raps on my door when he returns. I look at the piece of paper with Seraphina's writing on it. "Watch yourself" is what comes out of my mouth. "You don't know this woman."

I've apparently surprised him. "Mom. I think we can trust her," he offers.

"Of course you do."

"What does that mean?"

I'm not up to the complexity of that conversation this morning. I pocket the address, and say, "We need to get going."

Shortly after 10:00 a.m., the bright blue sky is filling with patches of dark swollen clouds that suffocate the air with a steamy pressure. I open my jacket and wipe my throat while Oliver rings the buzzer at Moreau's gate. The house sits on a lavender- and thyme-filled hillside on the south side of town, not far from our pension or the ancient baths of supposed healing warm springs. A tall stucco wall obscures everything about the house except its terra-cotta tiled roof. Is this all Mrs. Moreau's doing? How else could they afford such a place?

A woman's voice through the intercom, "*Bonjour?*"

"*Bonjour,*" Oliver says. "*Parlez-vous anglais?*"

"Who is this?" she says, haltingly.

"We're looking for Inspector Moreau," Oliver says. A pause.

"He has an office at the center of town. If you please. You may visit him there."

"Has he returned yet from Zurich?" I lean in and ask.

"*Pardon?*"

"My name is Celia Hagen. He came to see me in Zurich, and I was hoping—"

The wide iron gate buzzes, and then opens with a moaning racket.

Oliver and I share a look.

The gate clangs and locks behind us as we head in.

The driveway is steep, made of cobblestones set in a series of arched patterns. Plane trees shade both sides. I'm quickly winded.

As I catch my breath, Oliver says, "I stayed up reading through the police notes before bed. There's something there. I feel it. I just can't see it yet."

I so want to believe he's right, but I've thought this myself all week and my faith is thinning.

A quiet moment passes between us.

"I called Benicio this morning," Oliver says.

"Did you?"

"Yes. Benny's been gone a week. Today."

"I know." I feel my hands balling up inside my pockets. "Let me guess. No call for ransom, no call of any kind?"

Oliver shakes his head. "I said I'd give him updates every few hours. He's worried sick about you."

"Yes. Well."

Oliver shakes his head at the ground.

The Moreau estate rises up before us. I'm guessing seventeenth, maybe eighteenth century. Clean white stucco, a dozen white-paned windows winged by green shutters. A fountain in the center of the lawn dribbles water from a seal's upturned face. The tip of his nose is gone.

The double doors swing open and out comes a tall, lean woman. Richly brown shoulder-length hair, long bangs, bright blue eyes that catch the light in the same way the house does. Her outfit is simple, elegant—white blouse and capri jeans, a sheer, silvery blue scarf wound loosely at her neck. I immediately understand that I'm in the presence of someone extraordinary, a woman of fierce intensity.

"Please come in," she says, her accent lovely, her English sharp. She stands back as we pass through the entryway—an open room with a parquet floor and bright white walls filled with paintings of all sizes in all kinds of frames, and some left frameless: Provence hillsides, terra-cotta-roofed houses, vineyards, portraits, most somewhat abstract. Her students' efforts? Could one be by the young lover Moreau told us about? One thing I'd bet on: none are hers.

I introduce Oliver and they shake hands. "It is a pleasure to speak American English," Madame Moreau says. "I studied art at Yale many years ago. I don't often get to use English in Saint-Corbenay."

She leads us into the front room, a long, elegant affair with a winding staircase at the far end. Classical music wafts about from an invisible sound system. "You're in luck," Madame Moreau says. "I finished working already. It's much easier to start early in summer." She rubs her hands together as if putting on lotion, but I'm guessing it's the residual energy from painting—I do the same with my temples and eyes after writing for hours, massaging away my alternate world for the day.

"Please," Madame Moreau says, pointing to the red wingback chairs flanking a marble fireplace.

We take a seat and she sits across from us on an oversize leather sofa.

"Would you care for some coffee or tea?"

I'm struck by a painting spanning a large wall; its jagged abstract cliffs and geometric shapes remind me of Cézanne. But after a moment, the forms take the shape of a man on top of a woman, in flagrante. I stop my eyes from giving away the discovery, but it's clear that Oliver has seen it too.

He turns and swipes his palms down his knees. "Coffee would be great," he says.

I nod in agreement.

"Alexandra?" she calls toward the adjoining room I take for the kitchen. The only other word I understand is *café*.

I picture Inspector Moreau living in these rooms with this woman. It's not the grandeur of the place that elevates the way I see him, so much as the atmosphere of love and art, of living with grace.

"We're sorry to bother you," I say. "But has your husband returned yet from Zurich?"

Madame Moreau leans into her chair. "No. In fact, it is only now that I'm learning where he's been."

"Oh. I'm sorry."

"No need. There isn't always a chance to share what we're doing. He said he would be gone for a couple of days…I forgot to ask where he was going. But he did speak to me about your case."

"Oh?"

"I'm very sorry about your son. Has he been found?"

"Thank you. No. I'm afraid not."

A young woman appears through the doorway with a tray of coffee, cups, sugar, and cream. "*Merci, Alex*," Madame Moreau says. "This is Alex. She helps me in the house."

It occurs to me that if I'd had steady help in my house they might've noticed something, maybe even *prevented* all of this from happening.

Alex shyly dips her head as she sets the tray on the coffee table. She appears Russian, perhaps Czech, strong cheekbones and pale, brittle arms. She quickly ducks into the kitchen.

"My husband is very upset with this case. He is… *consumed*?"

"Yes," I say.

I'm wondering if this is perhaps the biggest case Moreau has ever worked on. Whatever the cause of his determination, my affection for him grows.

"I appreciate what he's trying to do," I say. "He told me this man on the train may have been the same one who spoke to your daughter on the street some months ago."

"Yes. It's very frightening to think about it."

"He asked her…personal questions, your husband said?"

"A grown man speaking to a young girl by herself, in a familiar way—just that alone, but yes, he asked about her parents, he asked if she lived on the hill here."

"That sounds—" Oliver says, catching her eye.

"Yes. *Très inquiétant*," Madame Moreau tells him. "But it's what Arabelle said," she goes on to us both. "*I didn't like the way he looked at me*. Strong words for a child."

"*Très inquiétant*," I say after a moment.

She nods, mother to mother, accepting my stab at her language as a token of goodwill. "It's no wonder your husband is so concerned with this case," I say.

Madame Moreau again nods, meets my eyes long enough for me to understand she's working out the English of a difficult thought, or perhaps debating how *much* to say.

"Any father wants to protect his daughter, of course," she begins. "But, as well, his concern comes from his own *tragédie*, you understand."

Oliver and I trade confused looks.

"I see he didn't tell you this. I thought he must have. He's a man who, as you say in English, wears his heart on his sleeve. I love this saying. It describes him exactly. *De toute façon*, this story is no secret, everyone here knows…though it changes over time, I think, like *une légende.*"

She pauses to take a sip of coffee and motions for us to do the same.

I oblige, but drink so fast I barely taste what I've put in my mouth.

"When my husband was a child he and his younger brother, Rémy, were playing in the field near the train stop in Saint-Corbenay."

I glance at Oliver, then Madame Moreau. "We were just there. You mean the vineyard?"

"Yes, the old vineyard. It belongs to the Moreau family…well, to my husband now, though no one has touched it in many, many years. The grapes have gone to ruin."

I nod. "We saw."

The string quartet plays on. As I wait for her to proceed, I imagine Moreau walking through this door into his private life, and I have the strange desire to save him from whatever Madame Moreau is about to say.

She lowers her cup, and draws a long breath. "Something happened there that changed my husband's life, that put him on a different path. It was what led him to become a policeman, I'm certain. Rémy was kidnapped. The man tried to get both boys—my husband was older, just strong enough to get free, but not to save his brother."

Madame Moreau rises and retrieves a photograph from the sideboard, then hands it to me. Two young boys laughing atop a brick wall, legs dangling, both in short dark socks and laced leather shoes, both in caps and tweed jackets.

"It was taken just days before he disappeared. They were on their way to see their grandparents. They stopped for a picnic and the boys climbed the wall and waited while their father fixed an unforeseen flat tire. Their mother took this. It's one of the loveliest photos of two children I've ever seen."

"It truly is," I say, hardly able to stand the beauty, the weight of passed time.

Oliver gently takes the picture from me.

"Rémy was never found, not his body, not anything."

Oliver returns the photograph to Madame Moreau. She places it on the coffee table, facing her.

"The police naturally wanted to solve this mystery, but it became a very old case, a dead case, and eventually my husband's obsession with it made trouble for him. He used his office for his own purposes, they said. Last year, because of this, he neglected a case he was supposed to be working on…he missed evidence that led to his partner being badly wounded. The man cannot work—it's very unfortunate for everyone. My husband was able to keep his post only…because he is liked well, I think. He was ordered to do nothing more about his brother. But now, suddenly, here is the case of your son and it looks so much like the old case…Well, I know my husband. He won't give it up."

All I can do for a moment is stare.

Madame Moreau looks at us with sympathy. She says, "I know this is all…so much."

I nod, gathering my thoughts.

But before I speak, she goes on, "I'm afraid there is more to tell you. Since the time when Rémy was taken, other children have also been taken. Not in Saint-Corbenay, but in small towns like this one, in other regions of France. Many children. Dozens. And others from Germany, the Netherlands, Austria. No one knows how many. These crimes were so—" She waves her hand in a way I take to mean *scattered all over*. "It was a long time before the pattern was seen. And now, it appears that there is *un syndicat* devoted to stealing children."

It's as if a toxic gas has been released in the room and I've breathed a great draft of it in.

"Who *are* these people?" Oliver asks.

"There are only theories. Please keep this in mind. Do you know the Romani? Gypsies, they are often called?"

"Of course."

"The Romani live in an invisible way, in the streets, or just outside of towns, so one theory is that Romanian criminals use these Romani to steal children. It is the perfect crime, you understand, to hide them in plain sight. The Romani live among us, but at the same time, are not really there."

"I hate to ask, but what do they do with all these children?" I say.

Just then a young girl who favors Madame Moreau in nearly every way—eyes, hair, long, graceful limbs—bounds into the room and clasps her skinny arms around Madame Moreau's neck.

"Arabelle," she says, kissing the top of the girl's head. Arabelle peers out from her mother's neck, and then shyly tucks her face back in. Her mother whispers to her, but I've already turned away.

When I turn back, the girl is bouncing up the stairway, then disappears.

"I apologize. We have plans—" Madame Moreau begins.

"We won't keep you," Oliver says.

But I can't let this interview end too soon. I ask again why the children are stolen.

Madame Moreau nods and says, "Theories, you understand?"

"A theory is better than nothing," I say.

"Not necessarily," Oliver says.

I know he's right, I know how bad theories muddy the water; all the same, we need to hear this.

I look to Madame Moreau urgently.

"It's mostly girls," she says, "for marriages."

"Marriages?" I say.

"It has to do with *génes.* This is the same word in English, I think."

"Yes, genes," Oliver says. "You mean because of inbreeding?"

"Ah, yes. Of course. The Romani are a very closed population. Even their language, with so many dialects. Not many outside can speak it."

"But Rémy and Benny—they're boys," I say. This is making me sick.

"Again, it is only a theory. The children are taken for… more than one purpose. It is thought that the Romani slip back into Romania without being seen, and turn the children over to orphanages, who sell them to couples from the West, as Romanian orphans."

I think of Benny's coloring and how easily he could be taken for Romanian.

"This is big business in the United States," she says.

"No, wait," Oliver says. "I'm no expert, but Romania's in the EU now, aren't they? The borders are open? They wouldn't need the Romani—"

I'm still stuck at the thought of Benny ending up in the States without me. It's strangely comforting, and then more dreadful than I can bear when I think of how big a place it is.

"You're right," Madame Moreau says. "But this began long ago…it is perhaps a skill passed down to younger generations who continue this *work* because it is what they know. Again, I must say, this is a theory."

"But there's no shortage of real orphans in Romania, is there?" Oliver sensibly asks.

"Sadly, this is so, but many are…damaged. Sick, abused, many from addicted parents. Couples in the United States know this, they have these children examined by their own doctors. But the stolen children, with their bright eyes and healthy bodies, they are a kind of prize. It's a terrible thing to say. No doubt the orphanage comes up with stories of educated, well-traveled parents. The couples are so hungry for a child, the price is…"

She rubs her hands together again, as if she can wipe the stain of all this from them.

"I've heard as much as a hundred thousand dollars per child," she continues. "The couples are very wealthy, and as I say, desperate, and of course they believe they're doing a good deed, taking in these poor children."

"But Benny is way too old for this," I say, my wits coming back to me. "He'd remember where he came from," I say, "and of course he speaks English and German. And quite a bit of Spanish."

"We shouldn't assume this is what has happened to your son, Ms. Hagen. It may have nothing to do with your situation. But I thought you should know *le contexte,* the—"

"The background," Oliver says.

Madame Moreau nods.

After a moment, she says, "I've watched my husband live with this as long as I've known him. I know how difficult—"

"To go so long without knowing," I say.

Madame Moreau nods.

She goes on, "The Romani are always moving, they carry no passports. Their own babies never appear in any birth records—if they did, the government could step in and remove a child if they thought it wasn't being cared for. No one expects a Roma child to have any identification. And the ones who are stolen and taken to Romanian orphanages are quickly given false passports, adopted, and shipped off. This is part of the appeal for Americans. Quick adoptions. China makes them wait a year or more…and Americans feel better knowing the child has spent less time in a hideous orphanage."

"Have any of these children actually been found?" Oliver asks.

Madame Moreau glances at the stairway, as if looking to safeguard her daughter from what she's about to say. "Several who had been taken as very young children and raised as Romani… by the time they were found they were already twelve, thirteen, fourteen years old, teenagers—they were Romani to *themselves.* After returning to their real parents, they immediately ran away. Never to be found again."

"Dear god," I say.

"And the others?" Oliver asks. "The ones who were adopted?"

"There is just one story I know, and I'm afraid it is equally sad. My husband met a woman in London who discovered she was actually a child stolen as a toddler from France, from a lovely village in Normandy. She was so angry that her parents hadn't asked more questions before adopting her from Romania, especially after she located the records of her birth. She discovered that both of her biological parents had committed suicide several years after she was abducted."

It isn't until Oliver is in front of me that I realize I've slumped forward, apparently passed out, or something close to it, from holding my breath.

CHAPTER SIXTEEN

An hour later, I've convinced Oliver and Madame Moreau that I'm well enough to leave. Even so, Oliver stays close as we head down the driveway.

A gang of Roma Gypsies. This is madness. An ugly stereotype. Gypsies stealing children.

I pat Oliver's shoulder to comfort myself as much as him.

Do I take Madame Moreau's story at face value? It seems like something out of Ceausescu's Romania, or an even era much deeper in time. How much is *légende*? Could Benny truly have been snatched up by Gypsies? Is it absurd? Is it *not* absurd?

The gate clangs shut behind us. The tip of Mount St. Victoire rises in the distance, and I realize, for the first time, it's the mountain Cézanne painted again and again—all different angles, seasons, times of day, all with the telltale limestone jutting into the sky like a crude stone tool. How often I've seen it on postcards spinning in wire racks. But this is the thing itself. I can't say why exactly, but the sight makes me feel minuscule, a tiny human speck, helpless. I haven't often felt this way in recent years, overmatched and clueless, I realize—understanding, too, that if I give in to this mood I'll never get back what I've lost.

"Do you think Moreau meant to tell you about his brother when he came to Zurich," Oliver says, "but changed his mind?"

"Maybe he took one look at the state I was in—"

"Or maybe having Isak there?"

"There does seem to be tension between them…at first I thought it was about who was in charge, but maybe it's more than that. Moreau might blame Interpol for not locating his brother… or because they stopped looking."

Oliver steps around to the passenger side.

"I need air," I say, studying him over the hood. "Do you mind if I walk back?"

"Of course I mind."

"I need to think."

"Mom. You passed out up there. Get in."

"I haven't been alone in a week, Oliver. I'm used to being alone. It's how I work."

"OK, but it's not a good idea at the moment. It seems dangerous."

"In this lovely neighborhood in the middle of the day? It's a fifteen-minute walk. If that."

Oliver scans the street, the questionable sky. "It's going to rain," he says.

"Not in the next fifteen minutes, it's not." I toss him the car keys.

"If you're not back by then I'm calling Isak, Benicio, the local gendarmes, and the international press."

We stare back and forth.

"You think I'm kidding."

"No, I believe you."

He grips the keys tighter in his palm and comes around to the driver's side, opens the door but doesn't get in.

"C'mon, Oliver," I say.

"No, it's something else. I need to ask you something."

I don't like the shift in his tone.

He glances down the street, stalling.

"Ask if you're going to ask," I say.

"Who's Emily?"

"Ah," I say. I'm surprised it's taken him this long. Just the sound of her name opens up a gusher of images, glitz and flimsy dresses, furtive texts, calls, kisses in dark hallways. But my psyche immediately counters with a stark picture of an empty train compartment, empty in the horrible reverberating way a place can be vacant in a dream, as if it's the true consequence of that one word, *Emily*.

"You already know who she is," I say. "Emily Sandstrom. She played the comic store clerk in *In the Company of Harold's Daughter*."

"Wait. *That's* Emily?"

"Yes. And apparently she's still in love with Benicio."

"Whoa."

"What do you mean, *whoa*?"

"She's just—"

"Famous? Gorgeous? A woman who doesn't age?"

"I didn't mean it like that. She's just very different from you. She seems so, I don't know, sassy, young." It takes him a second to hear what he's said, then he hastens to add, "I mean, she doesn't seem like Benicio's type."

I give him a look. "Don't *delude* yourself."

After a moment, Oliver says, "But what do you really know about her? Aside from what anyone can read in the tabloids?"

I'm about to say, *Almost nothing*, then I realize I do possess one major detail. "She's the reason Benicio got involved with your father. Long story, but Benicio was trying to find a way back into the States. To Emily. To the life he had with her."

Oliver looks stunned. "I had no idea," he says.

"You were too young, it wasn't information you needed to know. To be honest, I don't think it's information you need now, but you're a grown man, and you asked."

He nods, still figuring out what to make of this.

"It doesn't matter, Oliver. People do things when their back's against a wall. Let's just focus on Benny, OK?"

"It seems bizarre, but maybe you shouldn't rule her out, Mom."

"Of *this*?"

"I mean, don't you think it's funny how she's come back into Benicio's life just at this moment? After so long?"

"I admit it's strange, but look, what Madame Moreau was telling us, think how strange *that* is, yet it seems far more likely, somehow."

"Taking Benny could be some crime of passion," Oliver says. "A way of getting back at a man she wants but can't have. People do crazy things for love."

"Don't I know it."

"And revenge."

I feel the mocking smile melt from my face. "Revenge like that's reserved for someone like your father." I look up into his eyes. "I'm sorry," I say, "but it's true."

"I know," he says.

"And as for Emily, she'd have to be extraordinarily clever, Oliver. Think of the logistics, think of the connections she'd need to have."

"No, I know," he says. "It's just maybe we shouldn't...dismiss her so fast. If this isn't about money, or about the Romanian gene pool or whatever, then it has to be about something else. We have to start considering—"

"The ridiculously far-fetched?"

"I'm just saying."

"You can follow the thread if you want, but all you're going to find is someone wanting attention and chasing after a man who belongs to someone else." Or *did* belong, I think.

He shakes his head. After a moment, he asks me if I'm sure I'll be all right walking back to the pension on my own.

I can't help rolling my eyes at him the same melodramatic way he used to at me when he was sixteen.

He squeezes me, and then holds me at arm's length. "We need to ask Moreau about the Romani."

"I know. We're in over our heads with that, Oliver. I don't even know where to begin."

He hugs me and gets in the Rover and drives away.

The last person I want to think about now is *Emily*, but I admit it's better than feeling helpless at the thought of Benny being funneled through the well-oiled cogs of an organization whose sole purpose is to disappear children permanently.

So I consider her at every roundabout, fountain, and linden tree. I see her head thrown back, fingers on Benicio's arm, laughing like a scene from one of her inane movies. What does she want with him? Years ago, I realized how much I'd been thinking about a lost love of my own—Seth Reilly—a man who ended up helping me when I most needed it. He's married now, happy, and I'm actually friends with his wife, Julia. My life with Seth is nearly erased from my senses, overlaid with memories of Benicio. But not everyone moves on, I know that. Not everyone has someone to make her forget the past.

I look up from the sidewalk and glance both ways. The street is too steep, the trees too large and green. It seems I've taken a wrong turn. A man and woman follow along behind me, chatting in a language other than French. Italian? I stop at a newsstand and let them pass. A small panic rises to my chest. I have no phone.

But I can't be lost, I haven't gone that far. I orientate myself to Mount St. Victoire, study the sky, which is more than ready to let loose a soaking rain. Sounds of the market square drift in from the west, so I head straight, two more blocks, and my chest finally eases with relief: there's the rooftop of our pension, just beyond a structure that looks like a small water treatment plant. I simply went a block too far in one direction, then several more in another. I cut across a small alleyway behind the plant, practically running now, as I'm sure the fifteen minutes Oliver granted me is about up. And, of course, I'm chiding myself for squandering my time to think on Emily, and I still have no plan.

I'm about to round a corner that will bring me onto our street, when I hear hard boot steps, coming up behind me. I turn just as a hand grips my shoulder.

Before I can speak, my backbone grazes a stone in the wall, and then a forearm, like a baseball bat, restrains me by the throat.

"Do *not* make a sound," the man says.

Please let it be my purse, I think.

I try to lift it toward him, to say it's full of more cash than he's probably ever seen in one place, but I can't speak, and his arm pinning my throat is only part of the reason.

He's the man from the train. What's more, English has replaced the French he spoke. And not just any English. *My* English. The man from the train is *American*.

I gag and he eases off, slightly. I stare at the shape of his closed mouth, the only thing I'd seen on the man who'd strolled by in the hat, the man who broke into my car and stole my backpack and computer. It was *him*, walking right by us in the middle of the day.

"Why are you doing this?" I croak.

He presses his arm back into me and sets off a chain of choking. "You need to stop," he says through his teeth. "You need to go home and wait."

I choke so fiercely I can't hear anything else. He drops his arm and grips my hair. I think to claw his eyes, and I could, I could just reach up and jam my nails right into his face, but I need to know who he is, what he wants, what he knows about Benny.

"Where is he?" I ask.

He shows the tiniest glint of something like pity, but it's gone in an instant. He says, "You have no idea what you're up against."

"Please," I say. "Tell me where he is. Is it money? I'll give you whatever you ask."

He yanks my hair and I yelp without meaning to.

"I said shut up." He checks behind him quickly.

We could pass as lovers backed against the wall, his shoulder obscuring my face. "This is bigger than you and all of your family's money," he says through his teeth.

"I'm not leaving here without my son."

He stares at me, hard. "We both know he isn't your son."

"Who told you that?" I ask, my voice fracturing. His grip on my jaw is so tight I feel his nails on the bone. "You should have stayed out of the way," he says.

"Is that what *you'd* do, if it was your child? Stay home and wait for a call?"

He lets go, abruptly, steps back just far enough so that if he wanted he could backhand me, and he looks as if he's considering exactly this.

"Please," I say, feeling my heart thud through my jacket. "I can't bear it. I'm his *mother*—you must understand that. I'm all he's ever known. I couldn't love him more if I'd given birth to him myself."

Again, his eyes give something away. An old misery yet to be fully wrung out. If I can just say the right thing fast enough, I know I can break through to him.

"You need to do what I said," he says, not viciously. "Go home before it's too late."

"I understand you don't want me here. I'm interfering with whatever this is. I get that. But he's just a boy. Tell me he's all right, tell me someone's taking care of him."

He seems on the verge of answering me, of saying more. I glance at his stained fingernails. His watch. "What is it?" I say. "Tell me."

The humane expression flees, another rushes in. Stony, practiced, annoyed. "He's alive," he says. "That's all I'm going to say."

He turns to walk away and I start after him. "No! Don't leave. I'll go to the police."

He stops. "Go to the police and I promise you he'll vanish and you'll never know anything. You'll spend the rest of your life looking at faces and never, *ever* see his."

I drop my shaky hand, take a step back, feel for the wall, and get my bearings.

Again, he turns to leave.

"What did you want with Moreau's daughter last winter?"

His body stiffens.

"Who told you that?"

"What does it matter?"

He marches toward me and grabs my jacket collar. "*Who*?"

"He did. Moreau. He knows it was you. They think I know you. They have a photo from when we were getting on the train."

He slams the side of his fist against the wall, says, "*Merde*," in what sounds like perfect French. And then, "Don't say I didn't warn you."

He takes off running in the opposite direction from the pension. I remain, numb, dumbstruck. Yet I believe what he said about Benny being alive. Strangely, my hopes are buoyed.

CHAPTER SEVENTEEN

The sky finally releases its downpour, soaking me to the skin. I race to the pension with the man's words roiling in my head. *No idea what you're up against. Before it's too late*. Just like before when he said, *What's the rundown on this guy?*

I bang on Oliver's door.

"Twenty-five minutes," he says, angry at first, pulling me in, then shutting the door. "What happened? You're drenched." He grabs a towel from the bathroom and puts it around my shoulders. "God, you're *shaking*."

I peel off my jacket and make my way to the desk chair, and try to dry my hair, but I can't stop shivering. I rub a corner of the towel around my eyes and the streaked mascara blackens it. There's a pressure in my neck and throat as if what the man from the train crushed hasn't sprung back open yet.

"The man who broke into the car…found me."

"*What*?" Oliver snatches up a box of tissues from the bedside and hands them to me.

I blow my nose. "You won't believe it. He was the man from the train. The *Frenchman* trying to help me find Benny."

Oliver's eyes widen. He backs onto the bed. "You could have gotten *killed*."

"Listen, Oliver, he was *American*. Not French."

"Really? You're sure?"

"On the train he spoke what sounded like perfect French, but obviously I wouldn't have picked up his accent. And, I mean, I was frantic about Benny. Then when he switched to English he had a heavy, very convincing French accent. Totally put on. The man's Meryl Streep."

Oliver touches my shoulder, looks at me like he might break down. "I'm fine," I say.

"No, you're not."

He gets me on my feet again, and sends me into the bathroom to shed the wet clothes. "There's a robe on the back of the door."

Moments later, I'm down to my underwear in the wan light of an ancient skylight, goosefleshed. My bra is uncomfortably damp in back, so I take that off, too, and put on the terry robe, one of the pension's few extras—that and, surprisingly, Wi-Fi.

"Better?" Oliver asks, when I'm seated again.

I nod.

"So..." he says.

"Moreau was telling us back in Zurich how the man on the train spoke in a way that reminded him of an English detective series he loves. I wasn't putting much stock in Moreau's tangents at that point, but what the man said in the alley just now makes me think the same thing, that it was coming out of a book, or a crappy movie. I got the feeling he was playacting, at least not a seasoned criminal."

Oliver lowers himself onto the edge of the bed across from me. "Did he see where we're staying? Do you think he followed you here?"

"He took off in the other direction, but who knows? Maybe he figured we'd go to Moreau's and waited, then saw me set off on foot. He found me *somehow*. Could somebody have told him we're here? Maybe he'd been planning on staking out the pension."

"We have to get out of here," Oliver says, and immediately grabs up his backpack and starts to stuff the few things he's gotten out of it back in. "And we have to hide the car."

The Rover makes me think of my missing computer again, and the fact that I haven't yet puzzled out what he—or they—want from it. But that will have to wait.

"Oliver, hang on," I say. "I'm not done. You need to hear what else he said. Sit, OK?"

Reluctantly, he drops the pack and sits again.

"I don't know what it means, or whether it's a hopeful sign or not, but he said this isn't about Benny."

"OK."

"He also said he and I both know Benny's not my son."

"Do you think this leads to Dad? Or Isabel? How else—"

"The part about Benny not being mine sure as hell does. But the rest, I don't know. When I said I'd give him money if that's what he wanted, he said this whole thing was bigger than my family's money. Not *my* money. I'm very clear on this. He said it's bigger than you and all *your family's* money. I mean, the Hagen shares belong to me—there *is* no other family. Even Benicio doesn't have access to it."

"I never knew that."

"It's true. But never mind. The man could only have been talking about the past, earlier Hagens, or the company itself. And the way he said it—it was as if I touched a nerve with the word *money*."

For a quick second I'm lost in the past, thinking of my great-grandmother Annaliese. She's the whole reason I have what I have. She founded Hagen Pharmaceuticals with my great-grandfather Walter. One could say she is the hand that feeds me. Was the man from the train somehow referring to her when he said bigger than my family's money?

Oliver stares past me for a moment, digesting his thoughts, then says, "Wait. Back up. What did he mean when he said it's bigger—*what's* bigger?"

"I don't *know*, Oliver. *It.* The situation, the reason behind all this. In other words, it's not about Benny, though obviously he's caught up in it, and it's not about the Hagen money, though that's caught up in it too."

I snug the robe and pull my cold feet up under me. "So what's bigger than money?" I ask him.

"A mother's love," he answers in a way that manages to sound both jokey and dead serious.

"Besides that."

"Family honor? Revenge?"

"I'm thinking of something my mother once said: *When somebody tells you it's not about the money, it's about the money.*"

We both ponder this a moment.

"There's the money itself," I say. "And there's how it was made and who made it. That's why his saying *your family's money* seems so significant. And, really, you should've heard the disdain in his voice."

"What about those old lawsuits?"

"Right," I say. "But according to Isak, they all fell apart, and his office checked everyone out anyway. One of them's even dead."

Oliver frowns. He gets up and has a quick look out the window. "Are you going to tell the police—the guy's right here in town."

"It's hard to see what good that'll do. Think how Petit acted. He seemed to have absolutely no interest in putting two and two together. What the hell is going *on* in this town?"

I'm just about to stand and go next door to my own room, when Oliver kneels at his pack and pulls out a steno pad and pen. "Let's get everything down while it's still fresh in your mind," he says. "Anything you can think of about this guy."

"I think I've already told you everything," I say. "His forearm was just about crushing my throat."

"OK, there was the accent, the *your family's money* thing, and the fact that the way he put things made it sound rehearsed or canned or something."

"I was scared," I say, "but at the same time part of me didn't believe he was really a thug."

Oliver writes. Then he says, "What did he have on? Start with his shoes."

"I don't know. I heard him running up behind me, just for a second or two, and I thought, *This isn't somebody in running shoes*. It was a heavy sound, leather maybe, with a hard heel?"

"Pants?"

"Jeans. Kind of darkish."

"Jacket?"

"It wasn't the trench. A rain jacket, I guess. Black. Kind of shiny?"

"Could you see his shirt?"

"No."

"Hair?"

"Still choppy, brown. I don't know. Nothing stood out."

"Eye color?"

"Still brown."

"Did he have any smell?"

"No, I don't think so."

"Try harder."

I close my eyes; replay the man's voice. "Wait. He *coughed* a couple of times. I think he smelled like old cigarette smoke."

"Good. That narrows it down to about 99.9 percent of all the men in town."

"Remember, he was American, though."

"Anything else?"

I close my eyes again, think of his fingers around my face, and I see the gold of his wedding band. "He's married," I say. "He had a wedding ring." I bring my hands up, half-consciously mimicking him.

"Awesome," Oliver says, writing.

Then I realize that the dullish glint I saw was to my left. "It was on his *right hand*," I say in a burst.

"Really?"

"I'm sure."

"So who does that?"

"Germans, *sometimes*. Eastern Europeans?"

He scribbles again.

"The woman on the train didn't say anything about a wedding ring," I say. "She knew what make his watch was, and noticed the stain under his nails, but not *that*. Is that strange, or not?"

Oliver glances up looking a little distracted, then says, "Ah, I wanted to tell you I did some research while you were gone." He tips his head in the direction of his laptop.

"On what?"

"Not what, who."

"The lovely Seraphina?"

"*No*," he says, but the mention of her name changes his face, makes him cross and uncross his legs. "Emily Sandstrom."

"Oh dear god. Can we just please drop her?"

"I did a simple search, and found a bunch of stuff. She's involved with some charities and has some other business ventures. Outside of Hollywood."

"You did all of this in twenty-five minutes?"

"Fifteen. Technology age, Mom. I know you have no desire to talk about her—"

"That would be putting the best possible spin on it."

"I know, but I need to tell you anyway," he says, and forges ahead before I can respond. "It's common knowledge that Emily's a backer of some restaurants—and apparently she turns a lot of the profits over to kids' charities. They're all, you know, mainstream—Children's Defense Fund, Make-a-Wish. Like that. I guess what I'm saying is that she doesn't seem crazy or anything, just the opposite, in fact."

I'm not sure what to say. After a moment, I ask, lamely, "What kind of restaurants?"

"Mostly sushi."

"I *hate* sushi," I say. Actually, everyone in the family hates sushi. Even Benny.

Oliver nods uneasily.

"I thought you wanted us to get out of the pension."

"I do," he says. "But listen. I clicked on a link for the outfit that owns the restaurants, the R. Sebastian Group, and there was a list of upcoming projects? One of them is on *Bildungstrasse* in Zurich."

This I am not expecting. I feel my whole head flush, feel a throb in my carotid. I stand and swing open the casement window, needing air.

"Mom?"

I hold up a hand.

"Are you all right?"

Rain blows sideways against the glass. I widen the V of the robe, wet a hand and swipe it down my cheek and neck, which doesn't help. I can't catch my breath, and the drowning sensation brings panic. Oliver gently turns me around, takes me away from the window.

"You're hyperventilating," he says. "C'mon. Straighten your back, long slow breath."

I close my eyes and try to breathe like a Buddhist as Oliver strokes my upper arms. The moment passes.

When I'm seated again, hands folded in my lap, I say, "Oliver, Benny's school is on Bildungstrasse."

"This has gotten so bizarre," he says. "What the hell does this *mean*?"

"It means *something*."

"Isak knows Emily was texting Benicio," he says. "They must've looked into who she is. And the thing in Zurich, if we figured it out, how could they not?"

"If they know, Moreau knows. Unless Isak cut him out of it. But he probably found out, anyway. Moreau has a…shrewdness, I guess."

"So why didn't he tell us?"

I shake my head.

"Jesus," I say after a moment, "she's right in our *goddamn* backyard—"

"I haven't even told you the last thing," Oliver says.

"How could there be *more*?"

"I said she's involved with several other restaurants—a steakhouse, some Mexican-Asian fusion thing?"

"OK."

"The website has a picture of her at the most recent opening. In Paris. Last week."

"Benicio was in Paris last week," I say.

"I know, Mom. I know."

CHAPTER EIGHTEEN

Was Benicio the one who first came up with the idea of taking Benny to Aix? Hard as I try, I can't seem to remember. But what I *do* remember is how supportive he was, so involved in the plans from the start. And then? At the last minute, Benicio had to go to Paris for research.

"I need to go to my room and make a call," I say, reaching for Oliver's cell.

Oliver nods and types something into his laptop.

I close the door behind me and dial. Benicio answers in a voice that clearly expects Oliver.

"What the fuck were you doing in Paris?" I say.

I don't wait long enough for him to not respond, before I say, "Tell me exactly *what* research for *exactly which* film? Every single detail. And go slowly. I'm writing it all down."

"What *is* it, Celia?"

"Was she there? And for god's sake don't say, *Who?*"

"Yes."

I'm going to be sick right here on the floor. I sink to the chair and squeeze the armrest. "And don't tell me, *It's not what you think, Celia.* If it's not what I think, then tell me what the fuck it is."

"First, you have to understand I don't love Emily, I love you. You have nothing to worry about on that score."

I hear what sounds like a long sigh.

He says, "I tried to keep this secret as long as I could, but now everything is so screwed up. All right, here's the story: After we met with Emily about the part, someone asked her how the restaurant side of her life was going, so she explained what they had in the works, and she said one would be opening in Paris. I jumped in and told her about Benny, and the more we talked the more amazing she thought Benny sounded. Then someone said, *You should let him think up a dish for one of the restaurants.* She said, *What a neat idea.* I thought nothing would come of it—it was just people having a drink and talking. And then we discussed the role again, and how she might have a conflict, depending on the shooting schedule—for what it's worth, I should tell you that Paul ended up giving the part to someone else. But as we were getting ready to leave that afternoon, Emily stopped me and said she'd just gotten the wildest brainstorm: Why not design a whole menu around Benny's concoctions? She said, *He could be the Mozart of food!* Again, I didn't think it was anything to take seriously, but she called me after I got home and we talked, and I talked with her partners, and we texted back and forth, as Moreau told you, and somehow it all went ahead. So yes, I did lie to you about Paris—it was actually a business meeting. They'd already lined up a space fairly close to Benny's school, which would be handy for everyone. Anyway, it was going to be a huge birthday surprise for Benny—and for you too. I know how hard you've been working with him."

I can see the face he's making now—that boyish sorrowful look he gets that morphs on a dime into openness, into love. My eyes sting as they tear up against my will.

He goes on, "So I went to Paris early, and then you and Benny were supposed to arrive and you'd see the plans for this wonderful thing, a restaurant that would cook the recipes Benny invented."

It's all so absurd. Laughter spits from my throat, the kind verging on mania. "For god's sake, Benicio."

"I know."

"If you'd only just told me," I say, shaking my head at the empty bedroom. But then I'm struck with the thought that it won't happen now, the wonderful restaurant…not without Benny, and the sickness washes back around me, a terror imagining life without Benny.

"Then all of a sudden Benny's gone," Benicio says. "And I couldn't bring myself to tell you. I couldn't bear to make it worse. And after several days went by, it seemed too late. I felt like Isak would accuse me of hiding things from him, and why bring everyone more pain—to have to think about his future—"

"It's all right."

"I love you," he says. "You know that. You *know* that."

Years ago in Mexico, when my own life was on the line, I had to figure out whether or not Benicio was telling me the truth, and I realized then, as now, that the tone of his voice gave him away. It rang true in the cavity of my chest. It wasn't just the words. It was the eerie vibration left behind.

Except, why hadn't I trusted it before we left Zurich?

"What's the name of your hotel?" he asks. "I'm coming to help you find him."

I hear myself hesitating.

"You can't still be angry with me," he says.

"I'm sorry," I say. "It's like a whole new round of loss."

"This is exactly what I wanted to avoid."

"La Moisson," I say, my thoughts still trailing behind my aching heart. "The hotel is called La Moisson. We're going there now. It doesn't seem safe where we are."

"Did something happen?"

I don't answer.

"Celia?"

"I don't know," I say. "Maybe you're right about one of us being at home."

"No, we need to be together. That's obvious."

He starts to protest, then, suddenly, I'm saying, "The man from the train just pinned me against the wall of an alley, an hour ago," and I instantly regret it,

Benicio stutters, starts one sentence, then another.

"He threatened me. And he knows where Benny is."

"What are you saying? Did he *tell* you where he is?"

"No. He said I should go home and wait."

In the silence I can hear Benicio thinking, *I told you so*.

"But you're all *right*?" he says.

"I'm all right enough."

"What else happened? What else did he say?"

"It's a long story, Benicio. Can I just call you back?"

"Have you told Moreau?"

"No. No one knows but you and Oliver."

"You have to go to the police with this. They have *resources*, Celia."

"They're not inspiring my confidence, Benicio. They don't seem to be aiming their resources at the right things."

"Yes, but that's all changed."

"Benicio, I don't want to stay on the phone any longer. Oliver and I need to leave now."

He starts to argue with me about the police, but I say, "No, wait. What do you mean by *that's all changed*?"

A small silver van drives past the hotel for what I'm sure is the second time, slower now than the first. I duck to the side of the drapes and barely make out the shape of two people in dark clothing in the front seat. I don't think they saw me through the rain, but I can't be sure. The car speeds up and disappears.

"Celia," Benicio says, in a tone that immediately tells me that he knows something I don't. "I've been trying to reach you, and I didn't want to make Oliver the middle man. Yesterday Isak told me…This is difficult to say."

"What?"

"A childhood friend of mine from Puerto Vallarta told my aunt he'd seen Isabel on the street, a couple days ago. My aunt e-mailed to ask if I knew this. I hoped it was just a mix-up, but I called him up and he actually talked with Isabel himself…she said she'd been given early release because of overcrowding, and time she'd built up with good behavior."

"Dear *god*."

"This all came down on Benny's birthday—that's why she didn't call, she was going through the release process."

"I told you, Benicio. I *told* you she was involved in this!"

"There's more. When I confronted Isak about it, he admitted that Interpol was behind her release."

"Why on earth—"

"To *watch* her, Celia. To see where she *went*."

"I *knew* it! I tried to tell you and all I got was eye rolling." I want to reach through the phone and strangle him. "What about *Jonathon*?" I ask. "Should I be looking over my shoulder for him too? He'll kill me, Benicio."

"Of course not."

"Why *of course*? Isabel was supposed to be safely locked away—"

"I think you're right, we should get off the phone," he says. "We can finish this when I get there."

"No, don't come."

Again, he starts to argue, but I cut him off. "You acted like I was just some hysterical woman. You shut me down in front of Isak every time I brought up Isabel."

"That was wrong. I don't know what to say. I'm sorry."

"OK, you're sorry," I say. "I'm going to hang up now."

But I don't, nor does Benicio interrupt the dead air.

Until finally he says, "I still don't believe she has anything to do with this. My aunt told me how Isabel's gotten support from the community this past year…she's turned into a kind of folk hero, taking care of other inmates."

"That's a crock, Benicio."

"She's called every day since his birthday."

"Oh, hey. Thanks for the update."

"I knew it would upset you."

"Good guess."

"I keep telling her Benny's out with you, doing stuff. I know she doesn't believe me. And now she's stopped calling."

"You're so damn gullible, Benicio. You're just lapping it up."

"I just think you're wrong, Celia. I think prison has burned off whatever spell Jonathon put on her. I think she's back to being the sister I used to have."

"You're insane if you believe that."

"So now it's me who's crazy?"

He waits for me to answer.

"I don't want you anywhere near me right now," I say. He starts into another defense of Isabel, but by then I've brought my thumb down to end the call.

CHAPTER NINETEEN

Oliver and I abandon the Rover with its telltale broken window and Swiss plate in an underground parking garage in Aix. We're in the back of a taxi on our way to check into La Moisson in Saint-Corbenay when I can no longer keep the news about Isabel to myself. I drop my voice, even though we've established that the driver doesn't speak English.

"This is great," Oliver says, looking relieved, if not elated.

"You're not serious."

"It's like a controlled study. She's contained. They'll have people tracking her. This is *fantastic*, Mom."

All I can do is shake my head. His faith in Interpol is vexing, if not downright naive.

"Don't get mad at *me*," he says.

"I'm not mad, Oliver." But I am. I'm mad as hell that two of the people I love most in the world are so goddamn credulous.

Oliver crosses his arms in defense, slumps against the seat.

The fields smear past under a sullen, drizzly sky.

After a minute, he tries again to convince me that Interpol's strategy is a stroke of genius.

"I'm not going to argue with you about this," I say, and hate how petulant I sound.

"Terrific," he says, and turns away.

Then his phone rings, putting a halt to further bickering.

"Number's blocked," he says. "Should I answer?"

I snatch up the phone. "This is Celia Hagen."

"Twenty million euros," a man says with a strong accent. German? Swiss German? I'm not sure.

"Who is this?"

The phone sounds muffled for a moment, then he says, "By Friday."

Three days.

"That's a lot of money," I say, groping for Isak's instruction on how to keep the kidnappers from hanging up.

Oliver leans his head against the phone at my ear and listens in.

"If anything seems suspicious, someone close to you will pay. At once."

"I can't just—"

Oliver socks me in the thigh.

"Do you understand?" the voice says. "Make a mistake and someone dear to you suffers."

"Where is Benny?"

"First the money. No more questions. You'll be given instructions. Be ready."

A short silence.

"One more thing: Your son Oliver will deliver the payment. This is not negotiable."

"No, I can't allow—" I say, but the man is gone.

"Mrs. Hagen. This is Isak Larrson. Are you still on the line?"

"Yes," I say.

"Stay with me. We heard everything."

I am too stunned to speak. I look at the back of the cab driver's head, his fingers drumming on the steering wheel to the beat of French pop. I've forgotten where he's taking us. I motion to Oliver, *Make him pull over—*

"So now we have had the call," Isak says.

I nod as if he can see.

"There's no way I will allow Oliver to deliver the money," I say. "They're asking for something they can't have."

"We'll work that out."

Only now does the number start to hit me. "Twenty million? Is this a *joke*?"

Isak doesn't answer at once, no doubt calculating how much he thinks I should be let in on. Finally, he says, "We'll wait and see what they say next and go from there."

"I'm afraid to screw around with them."

"Ms. Hagen, it doesn't matter what they ask for; we can make it seem as if we're giving it to them."

So now I'm imagining body doubles and marked bills, and I think the fancier they make it, the more room for error. How can I risk it? "Why not just give them *unmarked* bills?" I say. "I don't *care*. You heard what he said."

"They'll have no way of knowing the bills are traceable."

"How can you be so sure?"

"You'll have to trust that we know a great deal more about this than they do."

"And Oliver? You *cannot* let Oliver do this."

"I will meet with my colleagues and let you know how we're going to proceed."

I begin to wonder if I have *any* power here—can Interpol do whatever it wants?

After a moment, wishing I didn't have to, I tell Isak to put Benicio on.

"He isn't here. He left with a suitcase over an hour ago." He sounds irritated, or worse.

"I told him not to come here. But I'm sure that's what he's doing."

I ask about Moreau. "I assume he's on his way back here too?"

"This is my understanding."

Where does this leave us, then? The kidnapping is about ransom, after all…and always has been. Isn't this what we'd hoped for? Optimism begins to trickle through me. We pretend to give them money, they give back Benny.

If Isak's right about the bills.

But why *Oliver*? Is he just more insurance, or is there something *besides* that?

"We won't forward the next call," Isak says. "We'll have a vocal specialist speak for you."

Someone can learn my voice in a day or two? More diceyness in the plan. What if they ask a question only I could answer—something extracted from Benny? I'd much rather do it myself. But then I see what else is wrong here. "Hold on," I tell Isak. "It makes no sense for them to call the house in Zurich when they know I'm in Saint-Corbenay."

"And how would they know that?"

It dawns on me that Isak knows nothing about the Rover being broken into…which means that Petit didn't report it, or, if he did, whoever he told didn't tell Interpol. Not only that, I realize, Isak's also unaware of my attack in the alley, and *that* means

Benicio didn't tell him before he left. Benicio who insisted I go to the French police, mum to Interpol himself.

My head is spinning.

Isak asks again why I think the kidnappers know I'm not in Switzerland.

I can't bear to explain—to give him the opportunity to say I should *never* have come, he'd *told* me not to, it's possible my rashness has put Benny in worse jeopardy.

"Should I come home right now?" I ask instead. "He said Friday—"

"But he didn't say *where.* If he does somehow know you're not here."

"Isak," I say, "I don't know what to do. You heard him, my whole family's in danger, and I mean, not just us, but the cousins, Klarissa, Emil, all the kids—"

"We know how upsetting this is, Ms. Hagen, but you should realize that these are standard threats, nothing special."

"They sound awfully special to me."

* * *

Oliver and I continue to Saint-Corbenay, check into La Moisson, and begin the wait for Isak's instructions. The lilac shutters are thrown open from each of the hotel's windows, and it reminds me, eerily, of where I stayed when I first arrived in Switzerland seven years ago. The place where Benicio found me. And where, Jonathon, of course, found me too.

But Officer Petit is parked outside the hotel, keeping watch from a small, unmarked vehicle that looks suspiciously like a blue cartoon-cop car. It isn't much but it's something, maybe.

I've tried Benicio's cell four times in the last hour and every time I've gotten voice mail. He could be midflight to Marseilles, the closest major airport. Where else would he go besides here?

Hours pass with hardly a word between Oliver and me. There's no way I'll put one son in harm's way to save the other. It's a cruel demand. I can't let myself be maneuvered into a position where I have to make Sophie's Choice.

We wait.

Does the caller know where I am, or not? No, he *has* to know. The man from the train obviously knows, and he told me to go home and wait. If I'm at home, then the exchange will take place in Zurich, won't it? Meaning Benny's probably in Zurich already?

If they mean to return him at all.

I tell myself not to go there. To stay on track.

I glance over at Oliver, who is pretending to read a coverless sci-fi novel he found in a pocket of his pack. He looks composed except for his erratically jiggling foot. I have the urge to stick him on the first plane back to New York. He'd never allow it, but I can't help thinking it was a mistake to let him get involved in this at all.

I still don't understand why Benny was abducted here. And why make the call to Switzerland so soon after roughing me up and warning me here in France? There's a disconnect somewhere. A huge missing piece.

I get up and walk around for a minute, sit down on the bed with my back to the headboard, stare at the phone, then at nothing. There comes a moment when I think I've fallen asleep but realize my eyes never closed. I seemed to have been suspended in a terrified trance.

A siren in the near distance startles me. Seconds later, it's grown louder and is joined by another, and another still, until a whole chorus of quavering cries seems to be coming from the center of town.

I freeze at the window, the stroboscopic lights and klaxon-like sirens messing with my nervous system.

"Sounds like a four-alarm fire," Oliver says.

"What's *happening*?"

"It can't have anything to do with us."

But the sirens don't let up.

I cover my ears like a child.

"Mom. Hey. Sit down. I think it's near the roundabout. Petit's talking on his phone." Oliver pushes open the window but keeps his face behind the drape. "I don't smell smoke, but with the rain—"

"This town's not big enough to have that many fire trucks or police or whatever they are," I say, my ears still covered, my eyes squeezed shut. "Oliver, please. Get *away* from the window."

"Mom?"

"*Close* it," I say.

He does, but the sound radiates through the glass as if it's nothing more than cheap muslin.

Oliver kneels in front of me, lowers my hands and holds them. "I think you should see a doctor. You're at some kind of breaking point."

I pull away, suddenly unable to bear his touch. "Isabel's running around loose, Benny's god knows where, someone's willing to do god knows what to one of us if we don't come up with twenty million euros, so why would I *not* be at a breaking point?"

Oliver gives me one of the same patronizing sighs Benicio was doling out before we came here.

"Don't *do* that," I say.

He almost does it again.

Instead, his shoulders let down. He takes a breath. "You have every right," he says. "I just mean your body's absorbed so much stress, I'm worried." He tries touching me again, delicately this time, as if trying not to burst a soap bubble.

I nod.

After a moment, he says, "We have to keep things in perspective. They're watching Isabel—if she comes for Benny, they'll find her and him both. And the ransom? That's good too. It pushes things…forward."

"I wish it were that simple."

"I know," he says. "But maybe it is."

I try to relax the muscles of my face, but they seem to be losing their flexibility. "Well, maybe it's exactly what's needed. Maybe the mouse will lead them to the cheese," I say, more cuttingly than I'd intended. "I'm sorry," I go on. "It's just this place, the sirens, and everything, reminds me—"

"I know. Me too."

Of course. He was there. *Oh, Oliver.*

After a moment, he says, "I don't think it's a fire…I think I should go see."

"*No*," I say. "If you want you can talk to Petit."

Oliver looks past the drapes. "He's not in his car."

"Well, Petit is useless. He probably went to gawk, himself."

Throughout the hotel, doors and windows creak and slam. *Everyone* must be heading out to gawk.

"After what the guy said on the phone, I feel like they have their eyes on everyone connected to me. You're vulnerable, Oliver. Please stay here."

The look on his face makes clear he's going, no matter what.

"Listen. I haven't checked my e-mail since my laptop was stolen. Someone could be trying to reach me that way. Why don't we do it now?"

"Let me at least ask down at the front desk. They might know what the deal is."

I nod unhappily.

He opens the door and there stands Petit.

"Oh," Oliver says.

I'm on my feet. "What is it?"

"Stay in your room, please," Petit says.

He starts to enter, but Oliver blocks the way. Petit gives a half-irritated shrug and stands half-in, half-out. "There's been an accident," he informs us.

"What *kind* of accident?" I say.

Petit ignores me.

"What aren't you telling us?" Oliver asks.

Petit makes the face of an officious bureaucrat. "I cannot tell you what I do not know," he says.

Oliver shuts the door in his face.

He picks his jacket up from the back of a chair.

"Going out doesn't seem smart," I say, the weight of too many confused decisions bearing down on me. "What if we need to get out of town fast? What if he sees you on the street?"

"The man from the train?"

"Or the man who called."

"You're sure they're not the same person."

"Yes," I say. But am I? The voices were different, but how hard would it be to fool me? It's just that, all in all, it feels like we're dealing with a machine that has many moving parts.

"Anyway, how would he know who I am?" Oliver says.

"We have to assume he does. *Please*."

"What if whatever it is out there *is* related to us?"

"How could it possibly?"

"I can't imagine," Oliver says. "But why did Petit stonewall us?"

The sirens continue to wail. The entire Saint-Corbenay police force must be down there—which can't amount to much—plus some of Aix's.

Oliver stands, looking at me.

Then he says, "I'm sorry. I have to find out."

His journalistic instincts have taken over. There's no use arguing anymore, no use asking him to at least wait until Benicio arrives.

"I'll leave you my cell," he says, zipping the jacket, then working the sweatshirt hood up over his head.

"*No*. There's a phone in the room," I say. "*You* need yours."

"What if Isak calls again?"

"You could just stay here."

"I'll hustle back." He kisses my cheek, says, "Lock the door," then he's gone.

I move to the window, and soon spot his silhouette disappearing toward the blurry, flashing lights in the rain. For another few moments, I watch umbrellas bump and bob along the sidewalk as people make their way toward whatever catastrophe has taken place.

I return to the idea of a *disconnect*. If this business is bigger than my "family's money," as the man in the alley insisted, then why ask for twenty million euros?

Oddly, when I picture him again, I seem to be retrieving his image from the file marked *Faces I Know*. Is it just because that first day on the train seems so long ago—weeks, months? Actually, it seems to belong to another lifetime, or some parallel surreal dimension. Over and over, I told everyone I'd never laid eyes on him before, but now my dead certainty seems to have been sucked into the swirl of other questions circling us. Is he someone I've seen in the States? Is he *reminding* me of someone?

After a while, I open Oliver's computer. The Internet here connects at glacial speed. I sit skimming the papers on the bed, including the only independent description of the man, Helena Watson's, and I'm back to wondering if her omission of the wedding band means anything, and again I don't know.

I get up and check the window, then the peephole in the door, and see no sign of Petit either place.

With Oliver out of the room, I let myself entertain the idea that Isabel's release might be a good move, after all. But when I return to the computer, online at last, his file on Emily is up on the screen, and pretty soon I'm thinking, *Or am* I *the gullible one? Here I am lapping up* Benicio's *story.* Maybe she's keeping her real agenda from him. Maybe this is a long-delayed payback, made viable unexpectedly by having Benicio drop back into her life. Stealing a child takes a special kind of malice. You never know how much distance lies between someone's public and private lives, yet nothing Oliver dug up, or Benicio told me, suggests a woman tortured by her past. Her days seem full and open to scrutiny.

Looking at these images of her is hard, though—lovely manicured hands, skin, gleaming cascade of hair. I remember Oliver's words: *sassy, young, so different from you.* And I remember the shots of her and Benicio at the premiere of *In the Company of Harold's Daughter*—his arm about her, the two of them so palpably gorgeous together.

Nor is it hard to remember the story of his deportation, the sundering of the beautiful pair. It must've been traumatic, heartbreaking, to learn he wasn't coming back for her but had instead run off to Switzerland with me. What if the *entire* restaurant story is a fabrication, and he *is* sleeping with Emily again? What if he's managed to convince her he stayed with me purely for Benny's sake? *The boy's been through so much already—*

This is ridiculous. It doesn't explain the ransom call with its even more ridiculous demands.

I set the computer aside, stand, walk to the bathroom, close the door, and momentarily brace myself against the sink. Its faucet has dripped so long there's a rusty stain worn clear through the porcelain. I watch a drop appear, fatten, quiver, fall, then another, and another, mesmerized by this little drama. And all at once, a little membrane in my mind bursts, and I'm flooded with an icy knowing.

Helena Watson is the one who took Benny.

I rush out of the bathroom and go to the window and scan for Oliver but see only the same shuffle of strangers and dripping umbrellas.

I dial his cell from the room phone. Six rings and it goes to voice mail. "Goddamn it, where *are* you?" I scream.

After a few seconds, I try again, then clunk the receiver down, get up, and check the peephole again, but the hallway is every bit as vacant as it was before.

I'm shivering once more, arms and legs, in the throes of another adrenaline storm. It can't be true. It *cannot*. And yet I see it, I *smell* it. The gardenia perfume lingering in the train's washroom. An old lady's perfume. Who'd give it a second thought if they saw her walking by with a young boy? The elderly, like the Romani, living invisibly among us.

And Benny. I see Benny's eyes look up at her, so trusting. What boy wouldn't trust a grandmother if she asked him to come along with her, perhaps carry something or find her way? And of course she spoke English too.

Then what? Did she hand him off to the very man she went on to describe to the police, the American with the dark-stained nails? I see it so *vividly*. The two of them trading Benny back and forth, so that the man was free to help me look, and she was free to describe her partner who, by then, was nowhere to be found. But why Benny? Why *my* son?

This time I try Benicio but slam the phone down on his voice mail.

I dig through my purse to find Moreau's card. With every drawn-out ring, I think of Helena Watson's description of the "Frenchman." Having just seen the man myself, I realize she made no effort to throw the police off. Why provide all those precise details, accurate except for the missing ring?

I hear Moreau's voice, then realize it's his voice mail. "At La Moisson," I say. "Call me, *now*."

Once again, I peer outside. I dial Oliver's cell, and again, no answer. It must be impossible to hear in all the noise. I'm starting to feel trapped in this room. Afraid to stay, afraid to walk out. If there is anything I hate, it's feeling trapped.

Another fifteen minutes and still no Oliver.

I can't stop thinking about how they got Benny off the train. No doubt they hurried him off at the front where the platform ended, then around the engine, as we'd thought. But what about the people on the platform, the woman who'd fainted, and the others helping her?

Then I remember that they'd been holding up a blanket—seemingly to block the sun, but perhaps really to block the passengers' view of Benny. Could that all have been an elaborate charade—the sabotaged air-conditioning providing the context, the medical emergency ensuring the stop at Saint-Corbenay? What was it I told Louise Lawrence, the hypnotist? That they all looked like they'd come from Southeastern Europe? Romania?

I try Benicio again, tell the voice mail, "Call me the *minute* you get this." I turn to the laptop again and sign into my e-mail, thinking I'll leave a message for him there on the off chance that his cell is dead.

But an e-mail address I don't recognize in my inbox grabs my attention. *Mine@aix.Fr.* Sent yesterday, subject line *Benny*. With a paper clip icon.

Oh god.

My fingers hover. Then, without getting the go-ahead from my conscious mind, I tap, the e-mail opens, a photo begins to unfold. Millimeter by millimeter a blank white wall comes into view, the top of a white, triangular lampshade, a wall switch, then dark, wayward hair, mussed the way it is when he first wakes, then the top of the forehead, the perfect eyebrows, lashes, eyes. How tired they look. And finally, his mouth, a small smile curled on dry-looking lips. I touch the screen, his hair, his cheek, his chin.

My sweet boy.

How did they get him to smile, if only this much? He seems older, his eyes larger than I've ever seen, his lids heavier, a pale lavender along the edge. From crying? From lack of sleep? From *pain*?

"*What is it*?" I wail at the screen. "What do you people *want*!"

I don't recognize his shirt. Blue. Polo. Nothing he owns. The light switch behind him is European. Similar to the one in my hotel room. The e-mail was sent yesterday, though of course the photo could have been taken days ago. I don't care. My instincts tell me he's still in France. I believe in my heart that he's right here in this town. I scour the photograph and it is only now that I see the small line written in the body of the e-mail.

Never yours to begin with.

CHAPTER TWENTY

If not mine, whose?

Can there be any answer but *Isabel's*?

So the ransom call, is it strictly a smoke screen? Am I completely off base about the grandmotherly Helena Watson, not to mention the swooning Gypsy on the platform?

Why would the address say *Mine* if it weren't from Isabel?

I stare into Benny's eyes. *Where are you, sweetheart? Give me a hint.*

I enlarge the photograph. Here's the corner of something, a kitchen table, maybe…a small blurry box, a can the size of a Progresso soup can, a jar that looks an awful lot like the one mustard came in at the farmer's market.

Please give him back to us, I write. *We're all the family he's ever known. I will give you EVERYTHING you ask in return.*

I hit *send* and the e-mail immediately bounces back as undeliverable.

Outside, the damn sirens will *not* let up. I'm back to being mad at Oliver—he shouldn't have left me alone, he should've run straight over and straight back. I'm about to dial his cell again when the phone rings beneath my hand.

"Where *are* you?" I shout, almost breathless.

"Brace yourself, my dear," Moreau says. "This will not be easy."

CHAPTER TWENTY-ONE

One night last winter, when Benny was sound asleep in his bed and the whole town was swaddled in new snow and the moon angled through our tall, frost-crystaled windows, Benicio and I were in the front room enjoying a late dinner alone. He unexpectedly got up and put on a CD by a French hip-hop artist I'd never heard of. He took my hand and pulled me to the floor. "For research," he said to the thumping beat, the singsongy pulse of urban French poetry. "No, seriously," he said.

He slipped off his shirt, tossed it to the sofa, and began strutting and hip-thrusting, two fingers jabbing the air. Then he was grabbing his crotch, going, *Yeh, yeh, yeh, yeh.* I fell sideways on the sofa laughing.

He pulled me up and out into the middle of the room and then I was shaking my own tail feathers, and both of us were laughing madly. "We're too *old* for this," I said. "What if Benny wakes up?"

Benicio didn't care, he danced on, playing the role like he owned it. In truth, we hadn't laughed like this in ages. I began to remember why the young found dirty dancing so appealing.

When I got my breath, I asked him what on earth he was researching this for.

"A romantic comedy set in Paris," he said.

"About star-crossed gangsta love?" I asked. "Or whatever the Frenchies call it."

"*Oui*, mothafucka," he said, and then we were goners, totally at the mercy of our own hysterics. Benicio danced behind me, his arms wrapped about my chest, and I remembered when he'd held me like that for the first time. Moments before his sister and their cousin Leon had come into the room where they kept us, Benicio and I had lain on the narrow bunk and he'd drawn me back against him, his forearms flattening my breasts. His lips brushed my ear, he whispered, *There is something between us, Celia, you know it, don't you?* Oh, I did. But then Isabel and Leon stormed in and Leon broke Benicio's nose with a sickening *crack* I've never purged from my memory. It bled and bled. I thought he was going to die. And yet, even after they'd tied him to a chair and left him, his head tilted back as far as he could get it, he still joked about the mess we were in, still tried to make me laugh through the pain and blood and fear, wanted to protect me, even then. How could I not love this man? How could I ever love anyone else?

Seven years later, Benicio is still so funny, so beautiful, so intensely *pleasing*. That night in the living room, we danced long after our food got cold, danced until our clothes were sticky with sweat and we could no longer stand to keep them on, could no longer stand to not touch one another. We fell naked onto the sofa and he whispered in my ear, "Who gets to live like this? How the hell did we get so lucky?"

* * *

I'm crouched in the backseat of Moreau's car, out of sight. His window is barely cracked; two feet above me is a slow-drifting canopy of Gauloise smoke. Outside is a chaos of flares, emergency flashers, searing white spotlights on portable standards. Every few moments, we jerk to a stop, then crawl forward again.

"So sorry," Moreau says. He takes an impatient, wispy-sounding drag, waits, slowly exhales, says, "People. Impossible to get around." He seems worn down, as if he's been awake since I last saw him in Zurich.

"*Les journalistes internationaux sont arrivés*," he says then, apparently to himself. It's close enough to English that I understand. He gazes left, right, taking it all in, his hands making little squeaks as he twists them on the wheel.

I force myself to stay down and not gape at the aftermath of what has taken place.

"How many times was he shot?" I ask, my voice so steady it seems not to be mine.

"I am unsure," Moreau says.

"But you *are* sure Oliver is safe?"

"I promise you. He is waiting for you at the hospital."

Moreau's English is halting, more measured than usual.

"Tell me everything you know," I say. "Leave nothing out. I need the truth."

Moreau sighs. "As I said, his taxi was interrupted by a car. No. Not car, a *van*. Peugot. For deliveries."

"What color?"

"Silver, I believe"

I have no doubt it's the same one that drove past our pension while I was on the phone with Benicio.

"OK, give me the rest."

"I can only tell what has been told to me. The facts often change later, you understand. But what seems to be true is someone from this car, this van, fired a gun into the taxi."

"And you don't know how many times?"

"We do not know. Not exactly."

"How many?"

"Perhaps three."

I know what it feels like when a bullet rips through flesh. I cup the scar on my calf, imagining the same searing burn happening all over Benicio's body. I imagine his breath growing weak. *Why?* "We did nothing wrong. They haven't even contacted us again."

"We don't understand it ourselves."

"And why should we believe Benny is all right? Why should we believe they're going to return him? These people are insane."

The e-mailed photo of Benny flashes before my eyes.

"Is Benicio really alive? For the love of god, don't lie to me."

"When he was placed into the ambulance. Yes, he was. This is all I know."

I see him doing his gangsta dance, wobbly with laughter. "Where was he hit?"

"They will explain at the hospital."

His soft face above me as we make love on the floor.

"*You* tell me," I say.

"His side. The ribs?" He pauses. "At least one in his head. This is what I was told, but as I said, these things—"

"I can take it," I say, holding my head, imagining Benicio near me, the warmth of his skin, and then the heat of his blood, his pain.

"We will find who did this," Moreau says.

"Benny is still out there waiting for you to find *him*."

Moreau grows silent. And then, "This was—*audacieux*? An *audacieux* act?"

"Audacious? Bold?"

"Very bold. Sorry. When I'm tired, my English…I want to say it is unusual to try to kill someone this way. Why did they not wait until he arrived at your hotel? Why shoot him in the middle of, *mon Dieu*, the square?"

"Have you talked to Isak?"

"No. Isak will not include me at this point. I believe he now sees me as nothing more than your minder."

I recall what Madame Moreau said about Moreau's disdain toward Interpol for never finding his brother. "I assume your wife told you Oliver and I came to your house."

"Indeed," he says.

"I'm sorry about your brother."

Moreau shifts in his seat, takes a last pull on his cigarette, and pitches the rest like a dart through the small window opening.

"I wanted to tell you I understand how you feel, if I may. The guilt. Like *un rocher* on the chest, is it not?"

I want to say, you were just a child. What could you have done? But *me*, I'm an *adult*, a *mother*, the one in charge. It is my *job* to protect my child…and I failed.

"These people knew I could never pull off what they were asking," I say.

"We don't have to discuss this now."

"Better now than later. We might not get another chance." This statement hangs in the air—I'm unsure what I meant by it. I pull my purse and Oliver's computer case closer to me.

"It is possible they are *amateurs*," Moreau says. "The train, this was *professional. Mais*, it is also possible they want attention. *Un syndrome d'Hollywood.* Possible, too, that something went wrong in the last minutes—"

"What do you believe happened?" I ask.

"What do *you* believe?"

It takes me a moment to form an answer. I'm still thinking aloud when I say, "I was going to say they saw his coming here as"—I take a chance and try—"*un provocation*."

Moreau does me the honor of smiling sadly. "*Une provocation*," he says.

"*Merci*. They may have thought we were disobeying the instruction, so they did what they said they would do. But I don't believe that. I think they wanted Benicio dead from the beginning. Dead in a very dramatic way, to send an even larger message."

"And why do you say this?"

"It's just a feeling I have…that it doesn't matter if I do exactly what they say or not."

Moreau turns quiet and I know he agrees with me.

"I'm being punished," I say.

"There is no one other than Jonathon or Isabel who might bear this kind of hatred for you?" Moreau asks.

"Their hatred isn't enough? Do you have any idea how manipulative they are, how evil?"

What seemed obvious only minutes earlier, Helena Watson's guilt, now feels crazily far-fetched. A little old lady with gardenia perfume involved in gunning people down in a public square? It's starting to really scare me how defective my judgment has become.

Moreau clicks his tongue. "Not easy to make such things happen from so far. And from prison."

"Only *Jonathon's* still in prison," I say. "Isak didn't tell you the latest developments?"

"Isabel has been released, yes, I know this. And I know, also, this happened after your son was taken."

I nod. "But she was allowed certain freedoms. Apparently, she's built a reputation for good deeds, giving money to poor kids in the town, and god knows what else—people see her as a hero of some kind, they've been rallying around her. That's not the Isabel *I* know."

"It would have been more *difficult* from prison—"

"So where is she?" I ask. "They're supposed to have their eagle eyes on her."

Moreau says he doesn't know.

"I tried to tell Isak. He was so smug—" He and Benicio, I think, but my anger at Benicio is an exposed wire I can't let myself touch. "He was so goddamn sure that looking at Isabel was *stupid.* Isabel and her perfect alibi. You know what? *Nothing's* perfect."

"And Jonathon," I go on after a moment, "in his fancy prison, like a private boys' school? Have you seen where they're keeping him?"

Moreau nods yes.

I recall Moreau telling Benicio in our bedroom that his errand in Zurich would only take about twenty-four hours. Now I realize he must've gone to see Jonathon. Maybe this was the real reason he came all that way.

We drive on.

Benicio, I think, *you are everywhere in me. How will I survive this?* But Benicio's voice in my head orders me to stay here, to concentrate.

So I tell Moreau about the e-mail. "There was a photo of Benny."

Moreau taps the brake, cranes his neck over the seat. "When? It said what?"

"It was sent yesterday, which…Well, they stole my computer, how did they think I was going to see an e-mail?"

"Is that not a computer in your bag?"

"It's Oliver's."

"You said nothing about this computer when we talked before, here or in Zurich."

"No, this was later—when the car was broken into, here in Saint-Corbenay. Petit didn't tell you?"

After a long moment, Moreau says, "*Oui*, I do know about your car."

"Good," I say. "I thought Monsieur Petit was just making scribbles on his notepad."

Moreau produces a faint smile. "Someday I will explain to you about Monsieur Petit," he says. "He's protective of me. A good friend."

I nod. "Did he tell you we saw who did it? We told him but he acted like he couldn't care less. We saw the man running off, only a glimpse, but Oliver and I had bumped into him earlier, leaving the farmer's market—we recognized his coat. Since then I realized he's also the man from the train."

"*Attendez.* The man who stole your computer is the same one who offered to help when your son was first missing?"

"Yes."

I see Moreau's head shake. Does he disbelieve my conclusion, or is he just marveling at the strangeness of the knot he's been told to untie?

But after a moment he surprises me by asking where I bought the stolen computer. I ask why it matters.

"Europe, or the United States?"

"Benicio gave it to me," I say. "He bought it about six months ago in LA."

I ask again why he needs to know this.

Again he gives me nothing.

"Well, here's something," I say. "The man from the train, who is also the one who stole the computer…he cornered me in an alley on my way back to the pension from your house. He got me by the throat."

At this, Moreau punches the brakes hard enough that I flop forward against the back of his seat. He grinds us to a halt on the shoulder. "What did he say? You must tell me *everything*."

This is the most animated I've seen Moreau.

I sit up, bring my cheek close to his face. "Please keep going," I say. "Take me to the hospital."

"Stay *down*", he says, almost hissing at me. He checks the rearview, then the side mirror. The icy halogen lights of a car that's trailed us shine on his face, making him squint fiercely. The car draws even with us and goes by without changing speed.

"Did he have an accent?" he asks.

"Ha! Did he ever."

"What kind?"

"You wouldn't believe me if I told you."

"American?"

"What else do you know that you haven't told me?"

He starts to respond but instead jams the car into gear and pulls back onto the roadway and accelerates.

"Who *is* this man?" I ask after a minute.

Moreau says nothing.

Then the car makes a swift turn and stops again. This time, through the rain-dotted window I see the universal sign for hospital above an arched doorway. I grab the handle, ready to dash.

"*No*," he says. "I'll tell you when it's safe to come inside."

We stare at each other a moment.

"He told me Benny was alive," I say. "And he said something strange about my money, actually he said my *family's* money. The way he said it didn't sit right with me."

Moreau stares straight ahead. I can see his jaw flexing. He rubs his forehead, then goes back to staring ahead.

Finally he says, “I must apologize for accusing you of texting with this man.”

“I wondered. Did you just make that up?”

“A tactic—Isak’s idea.”

“I guess I’m not surprised. Did you two know what Benicio and Emily were talking about?”

“The restaurant.”

“Why did you let me believe it was something else?”

“This I cannot tell you.”

“You’re using me…for something else, aren’t you?”

“You mustn’t share with Isak what I’ve told you.”

“Is that for your protection or mine?”

Moreau doesn’t answer.

“What do you *want* from me?” I ask. “Why did you want me to come to Saint-Corbenay?”

CHAPTER TWENTY-TWO

Seven years ago, I woke next to Benicio in a Zurich hospital. I'd lost a lot of blood and couldn't stand on my own. The pain was so piercing I could barely speak, let alone laugh. Benicio was worse off than me but healing steadily. As I lay watching him sleep, I was surprisingly flush with gratitude. We were *alive*, *together*, and even as violent as our beginning had been, I was going with the odds. It could only get better from there.

But now?

After I've waited in the car for an hour, Moreau sneaks me into the hospital through a locked side door. He plucks out the stick he wedged it open with and tosses it into the shrubbery, ushers me in, and snugs the door behind us.

Benicio has just come out of surgery, he tells me.

I concentrate on walking with a steady gait, counterweighted by purse and computer bag. Shortly before we reach Benicio's room, Moreau stops and puts a hand on my shoulder.

"I was wrong about the bullet count," he says. His face is stonewashed in the hospital lights.

"You mean you lied to me," I say.

"No. As I told you, facts change. You need to prepare yourself."

"Just let me see him."

"You have to understand—"

"I've seen things, Monsieur." I start to pull away.

"A bullet entered here," he says, touching his temple. "And exited here." He points to his forehead. "Another hit his chest, and a corner of his stomach and liver."

"I see." The fact that I'm fairly calm isn't lost on me. And I can see Moreau's taking note of it too.

"Another, the one that should have been *mortel*, tore his lung and an artery to his heart. He was, if you please, dead when they arrived. It took two *ressuscitations* to bring him back."

"Can I go in now?"

Moreau squints at me.

"Is there more?"

"Indeed. Though not about this."

"What?"

"It must remain between us. You mustn't let Isak know I told you."

"And why is that?"

"He forbids it."

"Does he? Is that why you're telling me? To show him he doesn't have jurisdiction over you?"

The tiniest of nods from Moreau. He says, "You cannot tell anyone, not even Oliver."

"I can't promise that," I say, starting toward the room again.

Moreau calls after me. "*Un moment*." He grips my arm as if I might fall. Or run. "You need to have this information. Please."

"Why?"

"I have my reasons."

"Why don't you tell me what they are?"

"*Non*. Not yet."

"Does this have something to do with your brother, Inspector?"

Moreau's eyes dart to the left. I've read how liars look to the left when telling their stories, searching the side of the brain where new information is stored. But then Moreau looks to the right when he says, "Benicio has been in contact with your ex-husband."

I feel a smile spread across my face. I know it doesn't belong there. I know it must appear menacing, but there is nothing I can do to stop it.

"Sure he has," I say.

"They were exchanging letters for some time through a post office box."

"This *tactique* is even more absurd than the last."

"All post coming in and out of the prison is read. The authorities were alerted to their communication. Your ex-husband—"

"You saw him, didn't you?"

"Yes. A man quite disfigured in the face, thanks to you. I have no doubt he deserved this, and more."

"I believe you went there," I say. "But the other, no way."

"*Que faire?* Ms. Hagen, this is the plain truth."

"I need to get in there," I say.

"Benicio sent him news a father wants to hear about a son. How his boy fares in school, his interests, his friends, these things."

Benicio would *never* do this. He wouldn't engage Jonathon, wouldn't betray our family this way.

"OK. Let's say there really were letters. How do you know they were from Benicio? Someone could easily impersonate him through the mail."

"But who would know these things about the boy?"

"Boys are boys. Anyone could have made up anything. Jonathon wouldn't know the difference."

"No boy is like Benny."

This is true.

"Naturally, we had the same suspicions. We have other proof, I'm afraid."

I shake my head, tell him, "No. I'm going to see Benicio now."

"He sent a photograph of Benny."

For a moment, Moreau and I simply look each other in the eye.

"Your handwriting was on the back, according to the prison. Your ex-husband is a bit of a celebrity. Everyone knows his story. And yours—your novel is very popular at this…private boys' school. The post inspector remembers clearly the photograph with your writing on the back, or at least someone writing in the American fashion, a woman's hand."

I must have swayed. Moreau has taken hold of my arm.

"A photograph with a date of June," he says. "This is all according to the inspector at the prison. Your ex-husband claims not to have seen it, and a search of his cell found nothing."

I shake off Moreau's hand.

"Perhaps you should sit," he says.

"No, I'm fine."

"We don't know what significance this photograph has," he says. "There are many leads, and every one could lead to a hundred more. But this, now, the timing is very suspicious."

I nod, knowing exactly which picture he's talking about. It's right here in the pocket of my coat.

CHAPTER TWENTY-THREE

A bank of monitors, color-coded cables, IV drips on stands…I don't recognize the man I've loved for seven years. It could be anyone in this bed. Head swollen beyond what would seem humanly possible. Bloody gauze everywhere. Chest pulling for air, helped by the oxygen forced down his throat.

Oliver stands near the bed, his eyes glazed in shock. He greets me with a quick, fierce embrace. Over his shoulder, I see Seraphina in a corner chair. She rises, offers me a sympathetic smile, and gently takes my things and sets them on a table.

A young doctor with thin facial hair and thin wire glasses barely glances up from his clipboard while a female nurse rattles off French he appears to be writing down. The room smells like blood, raw tissue, fear.

They must have seen him leave Zurich, must have followed him all the way here.

Somewhere I find the strength to step closer to Benicio, but I am frightened by the feel of his chilled pale hand, made paler by dried blood in the creases of his skin. Someone has attempted to wipe it clean, and removed his bloodstained clothes. Despite myself, I think of my bloody fight with Jonathon, his flesh beneath my fingers, the sound it made when I bore down and wrenched the skin from his face.

All the times we discussed Jonathon, all Benicio's fidgeting and pacing suddenly takes on new meaning. What I understood to be a general indignation over what Jonathon had done to us, now seems closer to pangs of conscience for hiding what was going on behind my back. I can't begin to imagine how or why Benicio would engage Jonathon about anything, especially Benny, whom he loves. What in the world made him take that first step?

A plastic Ziploc bag containing Benicio's wallet and phone lies on the side table. Small smears of blood cover that too. The police must have overlooked it as evidence in the chaos of the crime.

It's a miracle he's breathing, even with assistance. Do I really get what I mean by this? That he should already be dead?

Oliver pats my back.

"I told him to stay home," I say.

I feel so strange, as if my limbs are floating, as if everything's become insubstantial and I might suddenly drift through the walls to god knows where.

"Is he going to die?" I ask the doctor.

He turns, stares as if mute. "No English," he says.

"No English?" I glance at Moreau who quickly shakes his head. I throw up my hands.

Oliver has returned to Seraphina's side, and he's holding his face in one hand. He was in the square when the medical team slid Benicio into the ambulance. He was there when Benicio had stopped breathing. Apparently, so was Seraphina.

I turn to him, and say, "Oliver, I have to ask you something: What did your father say to you when you saw him in prison?"

He looks up, confused, frowning, even annoyed.

"*Tell me*."

"Not now," Moreau says, stepping in.

"Stay out of this," I say, and glare at him until he finally backs off.

"I don't have time for games, Oliver. None of us does. Tell me what your father said."

"That was so long ago."

"*Soll ich weg gehen?*" Seraphina asks. Should she leave? Her eyes are full of alarm.

"Yes. I don't know what you're doing here in the first place."

"*Mom*. Stop. You're upset. Let's go in the hall."

He touches my arm.

I step out of his reach. Clearly, I'm frightening him. I don't care.

The wispy doctor addresses Moreau in French. Moreau nods in return.

The doctor makes to leave.

"Where's he going?" I ask Moreau. "Where are you going?" I call after the doctor, who turns at the door. "You're a doctor. How can you not speak English?" I'm watching my disintegration as if from above. The drive to understand is primal. I don't want to have to think. I want English, and I want it now.

"He is from Poland," Moreau says. "He speaks Russian and Polish, and of course, French."

Is it possible to be slipping down the shiny chute to insanity if I'm aware of it happening? "And what does *she* speak?" I say of the nurse whose face is stark with fear.

"I have a little English," she says, timidly. "Your husband is *en condition stable*. His brain has"—she makes her two hands look like they're holding an inflating balloon—"*enflure*? But now"—she lets some air out of the balloon.

Why do I have the urge to crack up? Nothing is funny, but every last thing is ridiculous. Gypsies. Helena Watson, a goddamn Agatha Christie character in the flesh. I cover my mouth but laughter springs from my throat and the next thing I'm bent over, snickering, drunk with hysterics.

Moreau says something to the nurse and I hear her leave the room. Is he asking her to bring the straitjacket?

"It's *all right*," I say. "He's stable. His head is a balloon."

"Sit *down*, Mom."

Oliver's voice is like a blow meant to sober me up. How far we've come, I think, since I looked into this face the first time, his dark eyelids peeling open, his tiny pink hand slapping the air. Another of the hideous things Jonathon did to me was make it impossible to see this image of Oliver without seeing him there with us, kissing Oliver's head, gazing over it at me, either lovingly or in a flawless impersonation of loving—I'll never know which. I didn't give birth again after that, but the intensity of what I felt for Oliver, how could that ever be surpassed?

Then the line from the e-mail again: *Never yours to begin with.* I drop my hands. For the first time I wonder if I should just give Benny back to Isabel. What an ugly, awful thought. I'm not thinking straight, I know this, and yet I wonder if it came down to it, would I exchange Benny for Benicio? For keeping Oliver, *all of us*, safe?

The weight of the room, my body, my grief returns. "What did he say, Oliver?"

A wave of awareness seems to pass across his face—the look of someone just realizing he won't be able to keep his grip on a rope he's been hanging on to for dear life.

"What's happened here—Benny, everything," I say, "could've been orchestrated by your father. I know you know that. But I need to know what he actually said to you that day."

Oliver nervously wipes his mouth. His gaze circles the room, Seraphina, Moreau, Benicio, finally me. "I wanted to protect you. I thought, *This is something I can do, I can keep my mouth shut*, so you wouldn't have to think about him more than…you can't help doing."

"And?"

"He didn't ask to be forgiven. The stuff about the years in prison reforming him…he never said anything like that. What he said was that if he had to do it all over again, he would've…killed us in Portland." He glances at Seraphina, swallows, and looks at me.

The hair on my neck has bristled up like a cat's. I should have killed the man when I had the chance.

"He said if he'd gotten rid of us sooner, he'd be living in Aruba instead of a Swiss prison."

Moreau shakes his head.

"My god, Oliver," I say.

"He's a monster, Mom."

"Why didn't you tell me? This whole time…You didn't have to carry that burden. You should have told me, or *someone*."

"I did."

He glances toward the bed.

"Why would you tell Benicio and not *me*?"

"He wasn't hurt the way we were. The way *you* were. I thought he could handle it."

"All right," I say, trailing off. "I understand. I do. I'm not upset. I don't think I am, it's just…"

I turn and see Moreau at the foot of the bed, wiping his forehead, a strange, guilty look in his eyes. Did he know about this too? Was he lying about the photograph? What the fuck is going *on* here? If Benicio didn't send the photograph to Jonathon, who did?

Moreau seems to glance back and forth between Benicio and the lines on the screen behind him. He removes his hat and combs his hair with his fingers, more times than necessary. I see the gun on his hip, the strap holding it in place.

"You should leave, Oliver," I say.

"Why?"

"*Kannst du ihn nach Hause bringin?*" I ask Seraphina.

She nods yes, slowly, as if unsure that she has given the correct answer.

"Please, Oliver. Go with her."

"Why are you trying to get rid of me?" he says.

"Inspector, can you give them some kind of police protection at her house? I don't doubt that Seraphina needs to get home to her aunt, and I'm pretty sure after what's happened here that Oliver and I are both targets. Him maybe even more than me."

"Of course," Moreau says. "I can have them escorted from here."

"I'm not going anywhere," Oliver says.

"Oliver, please!"

I'm close enough to smell what can only be described as death, close enough to feel the vibration of the machine keeping Benicio alive. I want the impossible—to save him from that which has already happened. To travel back in time and wipe away the rancor of our last words.

And yet, the photograph. How to explain the photograph?

"I can't breathe," I say, realizing that I've started hyperventilating again, feeling my heart beating wrong, thumping and palpitating. Moreau looks alarmed.

"I need to step into the hall. I promise to come right back."

"I prefer you to stay," he says.

"Is that a threat?"

"*Non.*"

What is it he truly wants from me? I know he's picked up an echo of his brother's case in Benny's, and it makes me sad for him, but I have no resources to spare for that.

I think: *Is this how an asthma attack feels, like drowning without the water?* I wave the others away and step out into the empty hall, telling my body, *Not now. For Christ's sake, not now.* I slide down the wall and get my head between my knees and pull air into my lungs, cough it out, try again, then again, slower, understanding the paradox, that being strong in this case means relaxing every molecule of myself, and after another moment, like a switch being thrown, my heart resumes its normal rhythm.

No one has followed me into the hall.

I start replaying what Oliver just said about his father. Taking long slow breaths now, I make myself hold the words in my mind without flinching, make myself go back to the basic questions: *How did Jonathon manage this from prison, who helped, what did he have to promise in return?*

When I raise my head at last, I catch a sliver of a woman entering the bathroom down the hall. Small hips and dark hair rolling down her shoulders. She moves in a strikingly familiar way, her tiny hands quick, as if orchestrating the air in front of her. I think she saw me, but I'm unsure.

The bathroom door clangs shut.

I rise, carefully, and, supporting myself along the wall, make my way into the bathroom. No one is at the sink. I stoop to see under the stall doors. Only one is occupied—a woman with cheap-looking sandals, and small, caramel-colored feet.

I grip the sink and stand. I hear jangling, as if she's searching for something in her purse.

There's no time to think. I back out quietly and rush to Benicio's room. Moreau glances at me, quickly frowns. I'm about to open my mouth and tell him Isabel is just down the hall, but all at once I rethink the whole thing.

Oliver and Seraphina have stopped talking and fixed their eyes on me.

When I look back, Moreau is now studying Benicio while scratching the top of his head, a nervous tic, it seems, which pulls open his jacket and reveals his gun, the strap holding it in place.

The lights on the screen behind Benicio spike as if he's reading my thoughts. As if he's pleading for me to stop. Or begging me to hurry. I touch his hand and the lines spike again. His mouth twitches while the rest of him remains ashen and still. Under the guise of grief, I lower my head and think this through. I only have seconds and I've already wasted too many. How long does it take to leave a stall, wash one's hands, and, if I'm lucky, adjust one's hair or put on lip gloss?

I turn to Oliver. "I love you, sweetheart. You need to do what I said."

He starts to protest, and then stops. Seraphina stares at us both. They must sense the heat bubbling beneath my skin.

I know my strength is compromised, so I spin and shout from the gut, focusing all of my energy into the strike. My right shoulder crashes into Moreau's sternum, sending him backward. I grip his pistol with both hands and yank it free.

He stumbles to the floor, one hand protecting his head against the corner of the table. He's only half-successful. By the time he lands and I'm pointing his gun at his legs, a trickle of blood is sluicing past his eye.

Seraphina shrieks behind me. Oliver yells over her, trying to calm her and get me to stop at the same time.

Moreau has his hands in the air. He lifts his eyebrows and juts his chin out in what appears to be amused defeat. "You see, you are using me as well," he says.

"There's something I have to do."

"*Mais oui*," he says.

Seraphina quiets.

"What the *hell*?" Oliver says.

I tell him to hand me my things, holding out my free arm. "*Hurry*!"

Oliver loops my purse over my shoulder.

"The computer too."

"I need that," Oliver says.

"I need it more. *C'mon*. Benicio's phone and wallet, too. The bag, over there next to his bed."

Oliver is sixteen again, huffing while doing what I ask.

"See that they get the protection you promised," I tell Moreau. "Oliver, don't let him leave this room for at least five minutes."

"That makes me an accomplice."

"Right. Never mind. I never said that, Inspector. Oliver has nothing to do with this."

And everything to do with it, I think.

Seraphina presses the fingertips of both hands to her lips as she stares at the gun. "Oh god. Tell her I'm not a criminal, you guys. Apologize for me. I don't have time—"

"But it would be our pleasure," Moreau says, laying the Cockney accent on thick.

CHAPTER TWENTY-FOUR

I crash through the bathroom door at the same moment the woman comes out. Our faces collide, she shouts and fumbles backward, holding her nose. She garbles curses in French. She is not Isabel. Aside from her long dark hair and smallish frame, she looks nothing like her.

Christ, good work, Celia, I think in a flash.

"I'm so sorry," I say, slipping the gun behind the computer case dangling at my side. Did she see it?

She blurts again, her almost-black eyes burning.

"*Pardon*," I say. "*Pardonez*?"

She seems to consider ripping into me again, but instead tightens her grip on her purse strap and storms off.

The fluorescent lights buzz like a rabble of yellow jackets. The air is clogged with chemical scents meant to mask the smells of bodies—I can feel my skin absorbing it. *What do I do now?* Time feels like a huge, desolate ocean I will never get across. Benny may *never* be found. The e-mailed photo could have been taken within hours of his kidnapping. The kidnappers have already shown what they're capable of. Benny could already be dead.

I stand like a harrowed ghost in front of the mirror. I no longer recognize myself…eyes sunk into dark sockets, hair ratted, clumped, a *gun* in my hand. What had I planned to do in here, assuming it *was* Isabel? Send a bullet straight into her heart? Or *torture* her like the most patient of sadists?

Any moment someone will burst through the door and arrest me. Moreau will have no choice but to throw me in jail now. My search for Benny is over. Benicio's life may be as well. For the first time, I get a stark shot of Oliver out in the future, alone, stripped of all family.

I backhand the pistol butt into the mirror, making a little knuckle of ground glass that radiates long silvery cracks. I strike it again, once, twice, then the whole thing crashes down around the sink, clattering and ringing to the tile floor, spattering me and everything else with a million knife points of light.

I snatch a large shard from the sink, weigh it in my palm. One swipe is all it would take, and scarcely any pain.

Could I do it? Is this what I want?

Why am I even thinking this?

What I want is a single fucking *trace* of Benny.

I toss the glass into the sink, take a quick look at my hand, and see that, small favors, I haven't nicked myself. I have possibly only a few seconds to get out of here. I nudge the door open with my knee and check the hallway. Two guys in scrubs pass across the mouth of the adjoining hall, oblivious. I secure the computer strap on my shoulder, and start out, but just thinking *laptop* jars loose what Moreau asked me in the car. *Where did you get the computer?*

Grab this thought, Celia.

Europe, or the United States? he wanted to know.

It was a gift. From Benicio. He bought it in LA.

What does it matter?

I come this close to letting it fall away, to walking back to Benicio's room and turning myself in to Moreau. But then I simply *get* it, Moreau's point. "Dear god," I say to the empty bathroom. The *GPS.* My American computer came with global positioning software. It can be *traced.* I can find the goddamn computer within *minutes.*

And with it, Benny.

CHAPTER TWENTY-FIVE

"Surprise!" Benicio said as he set the box on the kitchen table. "Look what I brought home from your motherland."

"Honey. First of all, Switzerland is my motherland. The US is more like the daughterland. And second of all, you didn't have to do that."

"You mean you didn't want me to."

"I like my old computer. It works fine."

"You can take the woman out of the middle class, but you can't take the middle class out of the woman."

"You didn't have to do this," I said, even as I pulled it out and ran my fingertips over its glossy cover.

"It's *thin*," I said.

"Mm-hmm." He leaned across the table and kissed me softly. He started to pull back and I kissed him again. "Yum. I missed you."

He smiled. "You need to get over your resistance to new technology," he said, sitting down across from me. "It won't take long to learn the new stuff on this one. I promise you. And look at *this* innovation: the 'm' doesn't come loose when you hit it."

"Poor 'm.' I'll miss snapping it back into place every time I write *mime*."

"Or *mama mia*."

"Or *make me*," I said.

"Or *make mad love, Mama*."

"Yes. That especially."

"And if it ever goes missing, it's got GPS, like the car—you can track it. I already put the serial number into a website so check your e-mail."

"Serious overkill, seeing as I hardly leave the house."

"Yes, well, you never know. I like to be prepared. They don't call me the man for every occasion for nothing."

"You're confusing yourself with MacGyver."

"MacGyver, another word you can now spell correctly on the first try. And don't forget, MacGyver's got nothing on me. Watch me make a rope out of an eyelash."

"All right, funny man," I said, as the computer turned on. "It's actually very pretty." I tapped the keys. "Thank you for thinking of me."

He kissed my forehead as he rose from the table. "Brought to you by the letter *m*."

* * *

That night I hide in the backseat of my Rover in the parking garage in Aix. No Internet or phone service belowground—I just have to wait. I manage three hours of sleep before the nightmares begin. After that, I stay awake watching rats. Their muddy brown coats are a ghoulish green in the yellow light. They scatter beneath cars, scurry up and over garbage bins. I bang my foot on the floorboard every few minutes at the thought of one crawling into the engine and then, what do I know, finding its way into the cab. But they disappear with the sun; not long after, the town comes to life, and so do I.

Years ago, Benicio taught me the art of hiding in plain sight. In Mexico, it took a pair of flip-flops, sunglasses, and a purse from a discount store. In Zurich, a scarf around my neck made me look casual and local. Here in Aix, I pull my hair into a severe bun, make myself up like a model, and enter a high-end store on the Cours Mirabeau where I pay cash for a gaudy golden thigh-length jacket and matching heels. I throw in a necklace and froufrou earrings I wouldn't be caught dead in, and the irony's not lost on me—that I may very well die in this getup. Lastly, I buy a zebra-print suitcase in which I stash my old shoes and jacket, along with Oliver's computer. The gun and the rest of my cash shift around inside my purse as I strut down the boulevard feeling cheap.

The sky is high and clear, the temperature climbing steadily. I check into Hotel Saint Victoire without incident. It's true what they say about money talking—I offer to pay the week up front in cash; the fake name I give, Emily Watson, is taken as good; and a room key is placed in my hand.

I set up shop in a suite that resembles a giant hatbox, the bed itself like a headpiece embellished with satin pillows, its king-size quilt swimming with iridescent peacocks. I clear the mahogany table of the gift basket crammed with fruit and cheese and chocolates but pause at the chilled, complimentary bottle of pastis, famous not only for the 45 percent alcohol content but also for the lovely licorice flavor of anise. I've never been much of a drinker, but the feminine, blue-striped bottle and milky, soft-yellow liquid is so appealing that even the *idea* of drinking it soothes me. I crack open the cap, blend the liquid in a glass with icy water, and knock back a long swallow. I plug in Oliver's computer, and drink again.

Without warning, the liquor shoots to my head as if I've cranked open a high-pressure valve, and, *bang*, there's Benicio in his hospital bed, unconscious, intubated, his beautiful body savaged. A fit of bawling convulses me, thrashes me. *Let it out*, I tell myself. *Let this be your one good cry*. And so it is. I get down on the floor and wail into a three-hundred-euro pillow for nearly ten minutes. When this is over, it's like stepping outside after a long, hard rain. I feel cleansed.

"You people have no idea who you're *fucking with*!" I sing.

I take Moreau's gun from my purse, along with the blood-stained Ziploc bag holding Benicio's phone and wallet, and set them next to the computer. I toss my jacket from the suitcase to the bed, and from its pocket pull out the photo of Benny, which I unfold on the desk, where I can see it.

The Internet is a whole lot zippier at Hotel Saint Victoire. Way down in my stash of old e-mails, I locate the message containing instructions about the hidden software in my laptop. I log on to the site and follow the steps, which are simpler than I'd supposed. All I have to do is enter the password, then change my computer's status to stolen, and the search begins. A blue status bar gauges the progress. It seems stuck on 2 percent, but I'm encouraged that it moves at all. Any second, photos, screenshots, a satellite map pinpointing its exact whereabouts should pop onto the screen. I cup my hands in prayer. Please let it be this easy.

I'm not too concerned about being followed, at least not by the *gendarmes*. Every cop in Saint-Corbenay and Aix must be obsessed with the events in the square. If I were a criminal, I'd figure this is an excellent time to commit a crime.

The buzz of Benicio's phone in the bag startles me. I unzip it carefully, but can't avoid the sticky feel of dried blood on plastic.

I accidentally drop the phone on the floor. I glance at the table to see my glass of pastis is already empty. That would explain the slow ooze waltzing beneath my skin.

Oliver's name flashes on the phone.

I answer, "Are you all right?"

"The question is are *you* all right?"

"I didn't mean to frighten you."

"What the hell, Mom. What are you *doing*?"

"Seraphina must think I'm insane."

I eye the computer. Eight percent.

"I explained about Benny," he says. "I had to. Where are you? Are you still in town?"

"How is Benicio?"

"Tell me where you *are*."

"Oliver, is he dead? Is that why you're calling—"

"He's still *stable*. Mom. Listen to me."

I place my hand on Benicio's wallet in the bag and feel something hard beneath it. I flip it over to find his small notebook. Oliver has gone on talking, but my attention's strayed to Benicio's notes. The sight of his handwriting, this intimate piece of him, starts me trembling. I skim through notes about work—"Move scene 7 to 9 and take out 3." "No more raisins." "Bring on Jake." Some things are written in Spanish—"*Ella no puede recordar sus líneas.*"

Ten percent.

Then, trying to rejoin the conversation, I ask Oliver how Moreau handled things after I left.

"Strangely. He didn't say a word about you. He had Petit take us to Seraphina's and made him stay to guard the house. That was it."

"Not Petit, *again*."

"I assume he's the only one they could spare."

"Benny. That worries me."

"Did you just call me Benny?"

"I don't think so."

"Are you drinking? You're *scaring* me."

"No, it's OK," I say. "One pastis. It's medicinal."

I hear Oliver's frustration on the other end.

Eleven percent. Perhaps this is taking so long because I'm in Europe and it's a different satellite system. Then I worry it's not actually working at all.

I say, "Do you feel safe at Seraphina's? If not, you could get a police escort to the airport and return to the States."

"Stop trying to get rid of me."

"Oh, for god's sake—"

"Listen to me, Mom. I'm twenty-four, I'm safe, and I'm just as determined as you to find Benny. OK?"

"Of course you are. I'm sorry."

"Petit actually seems to be taking his job seriously now. He's tense. Talking on his phone a lot outside the door. I assume with Moreau."

"Anything new on the ransom?"

"No. I tried getting in touch with Isak, but he won't call me back."

Fifteen percent. I flip through more pages in Benicio's notebook and then stop when I recognize recipe names. Yellow Tuesday Chiffon, Galette Des Rois, Potatoes a L'alsacienne, with two question marks. Benny's name is peppered throughout the page. A jagged lump grows in my throat.

"If you speak with either Isak or Moreau, please tell me immediately," I say.

"Of course."

On the final page in Benicio's notebook, I find a list of five names. All crossed off except the last one, Johan Donders, a name that sounds familiar but I can't quite place. Donders is a common Swiss name. Next to his name is written the word *deceased.* From that, an arrow points to the name Helena Donders. It's been circled repeatedly. Helena?

Fifteen percent, holding steady.

"I need to go, Oliver. I'll call you back."

I hang up and run a quick Internet search and immediately understand why Johan Donders sounds familiar. He's the last person who tried to sue me for the Hagen shares. He must be the one Isak said had died. Is Helena his wife? His sister? Is her maiden name Watson? I search images with both their names, and a photograph of the courthouse in Zurich appears. Helena and Johan Donders had asked the court to show leniency for their son, Pieter, who was convicted of the kidnapping and attempted murder of his girlfriend, Kristina Rossi, who has since recanted her testimony. Pieter was sentenced to three years in Gefängnis Zurich. I slap my hand over my mouth. The same prison as Jonathon. There's no way *that's* a coincidence. This was three years ago. He'd have just been released.

I check Benicio's list again, reconfirming that Johan is marked deceased. Isak said everyone on the list had been vetted and nothing was found. But why look any further at a dead man or his family?

The search has leaped to 60 percent.

I back into the bed, sit, and try to focus, but the golden light spilling down around me from the curlicued crystal chandelier makes me sort of ill. I can't bear the thought of being drenched in opulence while Benny could be starving in some dank basement, or worse. A warm, soured taste of licorice billows up into my mouth.

I call Oliver back. "I need you to pull together every bit of investigative journalism you've ever been taught and find out what you can about Johan and Helena Donders. They were a couple that tried to sue me. He's the guy Isak mentioned who'd died. I need this quickly, Oliver. I can't stress it enough. And do *not* leave the house. I hate to say this, but I think you're in more danger than I am."

"What am I looking for? I don't even know where to start."

"Start with their son, Pieter Donders. He served three years in prison with your father for the kidnapping and attempted murder of his girlfriend, a woman named Kristina Rossi, who, for some reason, recanted her testimony. And I'm pretty sure he was just recently released."

"Whoa."

"If something should happen to me, look into the witness from the train. Helena Watson. I believe her real name, or married name, may be Helena Donders. The police report says she's British, but she may have two passports."

Seventy percent.

I flip on the cable news. The first thing I see is footage of Benicio being rolled into the ambulance. I close my eyes, but when I open them, I see my own face, my author photo, professional, serious, so completely out of context with what's happening. There I am smiling in the corner while the ambulance drives away.

"Screenwriter and actor Benicio Martinez was shot multiple times in the head and chest while riding in the back of a taxi in the small town of Saint-Corbenay, France, this evening," the journalist reports. "The whereabouts of his partner, best-selling author Celia Hagen, are unknown."

I can't stop grinding my teeth. What if Benny sees this? Or someone in the hotel figures out that this woman parading around in the ridiculous golden jacket is *me*? Damn it. Someone from the train is certain to put this together. Someone is going to come forward and say, "My god, that's the woman who couldn't find her child on the train, and now someone has tried to kill her partner."

Son of a bitch. If the story about Benny gets picked up all over the news, we will *never* see him again.

I let myself have another small serving of pastis, feeling my lips quiver on the rim of the glass. The report ends and there's no mention of me stealing Moreau's gun. Not that I really thought there would be.

Eighty percent.

I shut the TV off.

By the time I look back, the blue line has reached the end. A small box appears, filled with the words *Device located. Check e-mail.*

CHAPTER TWENTY-SIX

An orange tip on a satellite map points to a spot at the edge of Saint-Corbenay. My chest erupts with joy, relief, and then a quickening of anger. I was right. God*damn* it. He's right beneath our noses. The street where the address is located is depicted as a winding white line, the area behind it a large block of green—I'm guessing a park, vineyard, or forest. A blue river winds through the green.

Instructions for activating an alarm on the missing computer are included in the e-mail. If I want, all I have to do is push a button and follow the sound. Easy enough. I close the laptop and pull the same e-mail up on Benicio's phone. The map opens on the small screen in all its portable glory, and I feel a rush of hope, adrenaline, fear—I am on my way, you son of a bitch.

I slip on my golden shoes and jacket, and shove Moreau's gun in my purse. I slap on my sunglasses, stick Benicio's phone in my pocket, and when I pass reception, give my best "au revoir" to the man behind the counter, he replies in kind. The doorman holds the door, bids me "adieu," and that's that.

Five blocks down I retrieve the Rover from the parking garage and follow the map toward my computer in Saint-Corbenay.

Twenty minutes later I'm *there*, cruising a cobbled street where all the houses are made of smooth, pale stucco, the shutters faded blues, reds, and greens, rooftops bubbled in clay tiles. My first thought is that it looks like such a *happy* street, a place where neighbors share wine in their gardens and play boccie ball on the raked sand pit across the street. I experience a little sizzle of hope—maybe the kidnappers are nothing more than a group of misguided people who've made a bad error of judgment. This was the vibe I got from the man on the train, wasn't it? But then I picture Benicio in the hospital again, the terrible insult to his body. *Misguided?*

Don't go stupid now, *Celia.*

I hang back, park down the block from the actual address, and toss my golden jacket and shoes in back. I put on sneakers, wedge the pistol into my waistband, and cover it with my blousy shirt.

It's hot already, no sign of clouds. The town square isn't far, if I'm remembering correctly. The street doesn't appear to have been disturbed by the shooting or its aftermath; in truth, it doesn't seem like much of anything has disturbed it for centuries.

I start on foot toward the house, seeing now that the green square on the map is actually a large open field behind the homes. The house at the end of the street, the one where the map says my computer should be, looks like any other. Blanched stucco, faded lime shutters, lace curtains, potted red geraniums in the window box. The door is glossy black with a tarnished brass knocker at its center. I check the phone. I'm practically on top of the orange dot.

Now what?

As much as I try visualizing how this is going to play out, I get no clear picture. All I see is the B movie version where I burst in, flail the gun around, grab Benny by the collar, and run out. This isn't the way things go in the real world, I know that. And yet all I have is me. And a gun. What else am I going to do?

I can't just knock. Can I?

The alarm. I can drive them out or distract them enough for me to come in and take them by surprise. It's as good a plan as any, the only one I have. I pull out the phone, find the e-mail, hold my finger above the button, squeeze my eyes shut, and press.

Within seconds, I hear a steady, high-pitched wail. I back against a hedge, just enough so that if anyone opens the front door they won't see me before I see them. I stare at the doorknob, waiting for it to move. The gun is at my thigh with the safety off.

I only hope Benny's been told this was all a game. That his parents are coming soon, that everything's fine. I imagine him running toward me, his face growing larger and larger until he's close enough to throw his arms around my neck. But seeing that, once again, I see Benicio. It's all I can do not to burst inside the house, gun blazing.

The alarm continues.

I approach the front door and peek through a small kitchen window. A tabby lounges on the wooden countertop, flicking its tail. It glances at me as if unfazed by a stranger peering in—so precious, it seems, is his opportunity to lounge in a forbidden space when clearly no one is home.

I turn my ear toward the noise. It seems to be coming from the back of the house. The gun wobbles in my jittery hand as I crouch along a small fence made of crooked, sun-bleached posts. I duck near the back door and wait. In the center of the yard sits an ironwork bistro table for two, shaded beneath an arbor woven with grape leaves. A neat row of sunflowers lines the property at the back, and beyond that, a giant field of tall dried grass—as golden and bulky as wheat never harvested. The alarm is much louder here. Through the back-door window, I see no movement, no shadows, nothing but jackets and a straw hat on coat hooks. I turn my head back and forth between the window and the field and realize the alarm's not coming from the house.

I bolt into the grass. The signal climbs in pitch the faster I run. I no longer hear my heavy breath, or the pounding in my ears. Please god. Don't let Benny be here. For the first time since he went missing, I pray that I *don't* find him—not like this.

I run until my chest burns. I start to make out a river through the grass. The alarm is incredibly piercing now, at the threshold of pain—how can it make such noise? I must be almost on top of the thing. I send the signal to shut it off, and silence bursts open around me, the sky seems to expand infinitely, and for a few moments, all I am is a tinny dying reverberation.

I can't help myself, I kick through the grass, calling, "Benny! It's Mutti!"

Straw rustles in the breeze. I push ahead. Then something blue. Cloth. Nausea grips me. I have the urge to run back to the car, escape before I witness something I will never be able to forget, never erase from my eyes or dreams. But I don't run. I can't. Instead, I fold back the grass with the tip of my shoe.

A backpack. *My* backpack, slightly discolored from the rain and sun. The soil around it reeks of compost. And there, tucked safely beneath it, is my computer bag.

My knees give like busted sticks and I go to the ground screaming Benny's name. I crawl and scour through stiff reeds, clawing at the muck for clues I know I won't find. However long I tear at the earth, it's never going to return me to the life I once had, never give me back Benny in the kitchen laughing on his stool, that little-boy laughter that brings a crystal-clear joy like nothing else, nothing else.

CHAPTER TWENTY-SEVEN

The sun has dipped lower in the sky. Grasshoppers bound over my arms and legs, a dragonfly above my chest hovers and darts away. I should get up and do something, but I have no idea what. I'm afraid to move, afraid to leave the quiet of the field, only to receive news that Benicio is gone. And Benny.

I don't know how much time has gone by. I guess I've been crying—my face feels tight, though that may be from the sun.

The ground vibrates. The phone buzzing near my leg. It's only now that I realize it's been going off for some time. I start to move but my body resists. Blood goes to my head in stages, like the *tick, tick, tick* of a tiny pickax against my skull when I pull myself to sit. My hands are filthy, my fingernails blackened. My knuckles are stiff and painful when I try to hold the phone.

Oliver.

"Sweetheart," I say, my voice wispy and strange to me, my cheeks tight when I speak. I lick my sunbaked lips and taste the salt of tears.

"Where have you been?" Oliver asks. "I've been trying to call!"

"Is he dead? Benicio."

"No."

"But he's going to die, isn't he?"

"It doesn't help for you to talk like that."

"Your father will be the last one standing."

"Stop this, Mom. Where are you?"

"And Benny?"

"There's been no news. Isak said three days. It's only been one."

"No, that can't be right. What day is this?"

"Mom?"

"We aren't getting him back, are we?"

"You can't think that way. Let me come and get you, and you can wait with Seraphina and me. I don't think Moreau has any intention of pressing charges. If you give the gun back."

"No, no. That's fine. I'm fine."

How many times have I had to say that in the past week? How many times has it been a shameless lie? I shift positions again and a different pain shoots up my arm. Suddenly I'm an old woman.

I realize Oliver's been trying to get my attention again. "I need to tell you what I found out," he says. "Can you *hear* me?"

"I'm here."

"I signed up on this genealogy site. They have birth and census records going back hundreds of years. I found Pieter Donders's grandfather—*Johan's* father—in just a couple of clicks. He was born Alexander Siefert."

Siefert? The name is another hard thump to my head. My maternal family's name. My great-grandmother Annaliese's name. "You've got to be kidding me," I say.

"Not at all. It stops there, though. I couldn't find out who his birth parents were. But remember the letter Annaliese wrote to her daughter, your grandmother Sonja?"

"Of course."

"Remember what she said happened to her when she was young?"

He's referring to the rape. I don't blame him for not wanting to say it. "Yes," I say.

"What if she wasn't honest about it? What if she lied about it? I mean, she said a child never came of it. But what if one *did*?"

My thoughts are a jumble. "You mean what if Sonja was actually the result of the rape?"

"No. No. Not Sonja. Someone else."

"Oh."

"The timing fits with Alexander Donders's birth. He was given up for adoption. Or rather put into an orphanage in a neighboring village. The problem is, he was never adopted. He lived his whole childhood there." The orphanage changed his name to Donders.

"People must have known who he was," I say.

"Which is likely the reason no one wanted him."

I feel a thunk behind my eyes when I rise to my knees. "What happened to him as an adult?"

"That's where it gets even more interesting. Or awful, I should say. He married, and had a son named Johan. But not long after Johan was born, Alexander was convicted and hung for the murder of his wife."

"Good god."

"And Johan was taken in by the same orphanage his father grew up in. You can only imagine how *he* was probably treated."

I sit back on my heels.

"It's awful," Oliver says.

For a moment, I'm lost in the groggy imaginings of loving and hating one's own child, of wanting him while not being able to stand the sight of him. Then giving him away and hating oneself for doing it. Did Johan know his grandmother was living in the next town over? Was he punished for the sins of his father, grandfather, grandmother? An orphaned son of a murderer and bastard child, the grandson of a rapist? Misery begetting misery, trickling down to us, to me, to this moment, battered and stunned, lost in a field, my own child ripped away from me.

"You have to wonder if Johan ever tried to contact her," Oliver says.

"I can't believe I had no idea about Johan. Our lawyers took care of everything. I didn't know any of this, Oliver. I never saw his claim. His case was thrown out like all the rest before it even got off the ground."

"Apparently, he was a laborer his whole life. He died of a heart attack while laying cobbles in a driveway not long after his case against you was dismissed."

"He should have been taken seriously. He was a closer relative to Annaliese than I am," I say.

"I called Klarissa."

"Oliver, you didn't."

"I had to. The shooting has been running on the cable news networks for hours now. It's not like I could hide it. Besides, I needed legal advice."

I rub my forehead, feeling the numb burn of sun. I can only imagine Klarissa's horrified reaction at Oliver's news. "What did she say?"

"What could she say? She wants you to call her immediately. She's been trying to reach you on Benicio's phone. As for the Donders family, the court documents are public, and Helena Donders's name is on every single one. Her signature tended to be at the top. In Klarissa's opinion, the person who signs first is generally the one driving the case."

"You mean she was pushing Johan into filing?"

"Just a guess. It's odd that she would be on there at all. How did you make this connection in the first place?"

I glance down and realize I'm standing, gathering my things from the grass.

"It doesn't matter, Oliver. I think she has Benny. The gardenia perfume in the bathroom was hers. I don't know exactly how she did it but I'm pretty sure that she took him."

"The perfume. It was in the report the whole time." He groans.

"It's their son, Pieter," I say but have to stop and swallow, my throat a sticky web of dry skin. "He's the one I worry about most."

"I know. Three years in the same prison as Dad."

I heave the gun from the ground. It feels heavier now. "But the man from the train," I say. "Is he Pieter? Who is *he*?"

"Could be. He's got to be someone who works with them," Oliver says.

"If we find him, we'll find Benny."

The gun dangles in my face as I shade my eyes. I have to coax each leg forward into walking.

"I went to Moreau with this too," Oliver says. "I had to."

My muscles are heavy, cramping as I fumble through the grass. I need water, badly.

"I have to go, Oliver."

"Mom?"

"I can't talk anymore."

"This gives Moreau something to go on," he says. "Some idea of how and why Benny was taken."

"But not the where," I say.

"Let me come get you, Mom. You shouldn't be alone."

"*Where is he?*"

"We'll find him. We will. We still have time."

I hang up, pocket the phone, and stumble out of the field with my ruined bags in one hand and Moreau's gun in the other.

CHAPTER TWENTY-EIGHT

If I don't eat, I will die. A simple truth, a fact, and yet when I touch my lips with a spoonful of onion soup from room service, I cannot make it go in. The smell, which I've always loved, is now bitter, nauseating. I drop the spoon into the bowl, and the clang hurts my skin.

"Sugar shorts from the Sea of Cortes," Benicio sometimes calls me for laughs. He calls me "lunch money" and "button Betty," too. If I'm dressed up to go out to dinner, he likes to mock that old glam-rock song by singing, "Hot mama, whatcha doing after the show?" Once, across the table, he stopped in the middle of a sentence, took my hand, and said, "You are *such* a snack biscuit, bunny babe."

I almost laugh at the memory. Almost.

Who gets to live like this? he'd once asked.

We did, sweetheart. And we honored it, didn't we? We knew we were happy at the time of our happiness. Not many people can say that. We'll never need hindsight to show us what we already know.

How the hell did we get so lucky?

"We're so far from lucky, babe," I say to the glittery ceiling. "I think they call this *fucked*."

He'd be upset with me, feeling sorry for myself this way. I can practically hear his voice in my ear—"I'm not dead *yet*, so quit making plans." With his voice in my head, I smudge Brie onto a cracker and manage to force it down my throat.

Seraphina gets updates from the hospital every few hours and relays them to Oliver who relays them to me. There's been no change in Benicio's condition. He should be improving by now. *Something* should have changed. But he remains suspended in the murky nowhere, retrieved from the dead but not quite back among the living.

He couldn't have sent Benny's photograph to Jonathon. For one thing, taking the whole frame off the wall doesn't make sense. Why not choose a loose photo from a drawer? Someone in a hurry took it, frame and all. It had to have been a stranger, acting fast. It's always the handyman on the evening news. But we haven't had anyone like that working for us in years.

Or have we?

I scramble onto the computer and pull up the article on the Donders case against me. What does Helena do for a living? Of course. Why should I be surprised? There it is—Johan, sixty-eight, laborer, his wife, Helena Donders, sixty-five, housecleaner.

I dial my cousin Claudia. She sounds stressed the minute she answers the phone. She's been watching the news. I calm her down enough to talk, and she tells me about the audit. I ask if she's ever hired a woman named Helena Donders to work for her. More specifically, if Helena Donders ever cleaned my house.

"Funny you should ask me that. That is exactly what the auditors wanted to know this morning."

"Tell me everything they said."

"I can't. They told me I'm not allowed to discuss it with anyone but a lawyer. I don't understand. My business is legitimate. I don't know where this is coming from. Does it have anything to do with Benicio getting shot?"

"I need you to tell me what you told them about Helena Donders."

"I never met the woman. Renata does the hiring. As far as I can tell, she's done work for us on and off for years as an extra hand. We've never had a problem with her."

"Has she ever cleaned my house?"

"I don't know. But if I had to guess, I would say yes, on occasion, she must have. We do background checks on everyone, Celia. What is this about?"

Bloodline. *This* is where Benny heard the word! *Johan's* bloodline, *Benny's* bloodline, the truth of where each came from, the legacy of their birthright. The children stolen by Roma. Benny stolen from Isabel and Jonathon, Alexander and Johan stolen from Annaliese. Helena *spoke* to Benny. Of course she did. And then he *recognized* her on the train. My god. He went with her because he *knew* her. She was in our house. She took the photograph from the wall and, most certainly, saw the train tickets tacked to the front of the refrigerator.

I hang up.

I don't know why they picked Saint-Corbenay in particular, but I'm guessing they chose the train, and France, to throw everyone off. As Isak said, the train had hundreds of people, many of them foreign nationals. It complicated the investigation, and it bought the kidnappers hours, days, a whole week. Had Benny been taken in Zurich, the investigation would have drawn on a tighter circle, fewer people to consider, the connections more obvious.

I can't put it off any longer. It's time to come completely clean with Moreau.

PART THREE

CHAPTER TWENTY-NINE

Ten in the morning. Today's the day. We give them the money, we get Benny in return. The call instructing where and how Oliver should deliver the money could come at any moment. I still have no intention of allowing Oliver to go through with it, but Isak has Oliver's phone number and I worry he might talk him into something without my knowledge. All Isak ever says is that they have things under control. He refuses to elaborate. It exhausts and relieves me at once, as if I've fallen into a safety net, only to be caught in the webbing, unable to work my way to the ground.

I'm making every effort to stifle my anxiety. Having Moreau here in my room is a help.

He smokes in the chair across from me near the open window. The giant gilded mirror on the wall opposite catches our reflection—anemic bodies drawn into themselves, eyes sinking into heads, a jumble of bones in rumpled clothes. We appear made for each other, a set of old, broken marionettes.

"You're going to lose your job over this, aren't you?" I say.

He laughs and takes a long, serious pull on his cigarette. He releases the smoke through the window as if he's studying something outside. And then he shakes his head at me, and I know it isn't an answer to my question but instead a recognition of his suffering, an agony not to be believed.

I open a fresh bottle of pastis. "Care for some?"

"If you please."

I mix two glasses and offer Moreau his.

"I have something to confess," he says.

"Just *one* thing?" I ask.

He grins. "I shall start with one."

I swallow the pastis—funny, I'd pass on a stick of licorice, but this taste is my new friend.

"I spoke with Isak yesterday evening," Moreau says. "Briefly. Because it happened here, he was forced to tell me: I'm afraid they lost track of Isabel."

I bang my glass onto the table. "You've *got* to be kidding me. How can that happen?"

Moreau's face says, *Interpol.*

He looks down, trying to decide which device for putting off the inevitable he'd prefer. A Gauloise, a slow sip of pastis? He picks neither, simply runs a hand over the bottom half of his face and says, "From what I understand, she is here, in Saint-Corbenay."

No shit, Sherlock! I think, as if I'm twelve years old. "Did I not *say* this would happen?"

Moreau shakes his head, clearly a judgment of Isak himself.

"*How*?" I ask.

"In the chaos of Benicio's shooting."

"She was *there*?"

"This is my understanding. Before then, she had made no… evasions. She seemed unaware that she was *en filature*. But then she disappeared among the emergency vehicles, skillfully, with design—"

"Son of bitch." I throw up my hands. "I don't even know what to say." I knock back a long swallow, too much at once—I have to wait for the burn to ease, and already feel my skull filling with a soft yellow cumulus cloud, despite which I say, "And that's not even everything you have to tell me."

"I'm sorry. This has not been our…finest hour."

"I should've followed my instincts from the beginning and stayed here. Why did you send me home?"

"It was before I knew your story. What happened in Mexico. And then Switzerland. After reading the report, I came to get you. More or less."

"For your own purposes."

Moreau pauses, smokes. "It's true, when I read your file I thought you might be an asset to finding out the fate of my brother," he says, his smoke blue in the shifting sun at the window. "I must admit I've lost a good piece of my mind over the years." He taps his temple. "I realize now the cost."

"Tell me you haven't focused on your brother at the expense of finding Benny."

"Finding my brother has forced me to search harder for your son."

I take another drink.

"I was confident you would take charge," Moreau says. "And your thinking, how you turn things around and around, the process, is different than our own."

"You mean as a mother whose child is missing?"

"No. Well, yes, of course. But often that gets in the way. You are on the outside, without training, free of *protocole*…or expectations. If one has *l'esprit vif*, an empty mind can be the best place to start. Madame Moreau taught me this. A painter may find a solution to feeding the hungry faster than an agricultural engineer."

I nod.

"And with your history of taking matters into your own hands, and your—I'm sure you will agree—fearlessness, I trusted you, I wanted to see what you would find. But I was selfish to put you in so much danger. I must apologize for this."

"There's no need. I may have ruined the investigation by coming here. And poor Benicio—"

"*Non*," Moreau says firmly. "You have not."

"I thought I saw her, you know. Isabel. At the hospital. It turned out to be someone else. But this is why I…borrowed your gun."

"You planned to shoot her?"

"Yes."

Moreau stares a beat too long before drinking his pastis in an even greedier fashion than me. He coughs into his fist. "And now? Where do we go from here?"

"This is the hole into which everything has fallen, Inspector."

His smile is the warmest I've seen from him. "The Roma my wife told you about. Ransom isn't their game. Not like this."

"Yes, I thought that too. But you still believe they're the ones—"

"Indeed I do."

"Why?"

"Johan's son, Pieter Donders, isn't the only criminal who spent time with your ex-husband. A man whose father is known by Interpol for having been involved in this form of child trafficking was there as well. Gunari Beeri. It's possible he learned a great deal from his father. Gunari became quite close to Pieter, according to the guards. He may have taught Pieter the family business."

"Was Pieter on the train when Benny was taken?"

"No. I don't believe so. But I never did believe that the person who took Benny was actually *on* the train. I always suspected it was someone waiting on the platform, or hiding nearby."

I nod again, all of it making perfect, and now obvious, sense. Helena took him and passed him off to Pieter, who was waiting outside, behind the blanket at the front of the train.

"Who cut the wiring to the air-conditioning?"

"I can't prove it but I would bet my wife's finest painting it was one of the men helping that *fainting* woman on the platform."

"I see."

"Gunari was released a year before Pieter Donders. I understand he had a private conversation with Pieter's girlfriend, the one responsible for him being in prison."

"Which is why she took back her testimony."

"Most likely. Isak tells me little. You'd think we were on different sides. He's very stingy with information."

Moreau smokes and exhales. The slow unfolding of this little ritual somehow calms me.

"I can't stop thinking about those children," I say.

"Nor can I, of course. The problem is, wherever they are, they don't even know they're missing. If they've been told of their adoption, it's with the understanding that they've been *rescued*."

"It's the perfect crime. Babies can't talk, have no memories, and cling to whoever has them."

"In the orphanages, these children have been kept separate from the others, given special rooms, attention, nutrition. There is that to be grateful for. They are the first to go and at a very high price."

"Like Thoroughbreds or greyhounds," I say. "Or truffle-sniffing pigs."

"Precisely," Moreau answers, nodding, acknowledgment that we're both addicted to finding the funny part of black moments.

Then he says, "But *this*, asking for ransom, shooting Benicio. This is something else."

"It's Jonathon, isn't it? *He's* the *something else*."

"This has been my thought from the beginning."

"Nothing like waiting until the last minute to tell me."

"Again, I apologize. But there have been many confusions about this case."

"How do you think he convinced these others to act for him?"

Moreau snubs out the Gauloise and leans forward with his elbows on his knees. "He knows your weakness, or at least what he considers to be your weakness."

"What?"

"Your love of your family."

"He wants to punish me," I say.

"He wants to *torture* you."

I finger the scar on my leg, realize I'm doing it, and let go. "And these people, they get my money in return?"

"Exactly."

"While Jonathon gets revenge."

"It would appear so."

"This is why they need Oliver to deliver the money."

"Isak will not put him in danger. I promise you this. I know him well enough to know he is up to something. He has at least *that* part figured out."

"But you still don't know what they've done with Benny?"

"No," Moreau says plainly, meeting my eye.

I lean back into my chair. "Thank you for not lying." I start to take another drink and see that my glass is empty and set it down again.

"And Isabel?" I say. "What's her part in it?"

"This answer is too obvious for my liking," Moreau says. "I think there's something more."

"Which is…?"

"I can't say until it becomes more clear."

"And your brother? You must believe he's still alive."

"On the good days."

"Let's stick with them, then. You must have ideas about where he is."

Moreau shifts, visibly uncomfortable.

"I understand he was three when he was taken," I say. "That's old enough to have some memories of your family, of *you*."

"My hope is that in spite of being told those memories were dreams, an orphan's fantasies, that they remained, and when he was older he came to believe they were too…*solid* to be dreams."

"Would you tell me about that day? How you got away?"

I know he won't refuse me. He rubs his thumb on his lips, back and forth, as if preparing for the words about to pass over them. "I did everything I could," he begins. "I screamed. I punched. I kicked. It was a single man. He had Rémy by the hair. Rémy was shrieking too, saying it hurt. So I stopped yelling, I went limp. It confused him, and when he tried to change his grip, I jerked away, and ran."

Anguish lodges in my chest—all I can say is "I'm so sorry."

"I hope, if he sees me in those buried images, he understands I was running for help."

We look back and forth, momentarily beyond words.

"You believe he may have ended up in America?"

"I do."

"Where do you think he is now?"

Moreau's head tilts sideways slightly, a tiny smirk appears on his lips. It's a look that means, *What are you, some kind of idiot?*

And then, slowly, I understand.

I lean forward and take his hand, lean farther still and wrap my arms around him. I see everything at once: The man on the train. His brown eyes, the shape of his mouth. I'd never seen him before the day on the train, and yet the second time, when he warned me to stay away, he'd looked so familiar. It was his brother, I knew. I'd been that close. I had touched the man Moreau has spent his entire life in search of.

CHAPTER THIRTY

My first question is, of course, "How can you be so sure it's him?"

Moreau explains about the day Rémy approached Arabelle near their house, how he shook the hand of a doll in her arms. "Perhaps he realized he'd frightened her and reached for the doll's hand instead of hers," Moreau says, and I have to stop myself from saying, "Or he was just softening her up, about to snatch her before she had the sense to run."

He explains that fingerprints on the doll matched those on toys his mother had boxed up decades ago, untouched until recently. Not even Moreau's wife knew of the toys or the fingerprints.

"Another drink?" I ask him.

"If you please," Moreau says again.

I fill his glass. "I hate to say this, but might this not be a case of the abused perpetuating the abuse on to the next generation?"

"What exactly do you mean?"

Why is he making me say it? "Your brother was stolen as a child, so he grew up to steal children—"

"There is no evidence that my brother—"

"Excuse me. I understand how emotional this is for you, but he pinned me against a rock wall and ordered me to stay away. *And* he knew where Benny was."

Before Moreau can open his mouth, the phone rings.

It's Oliver, his voice panicky. I set the phone to speaker so Moreau can hear too.

"The man from the market," Oliver says. "Who did the portrait of Benny…" He seems to be catching his breath. "Seraphina had to pick up her aunt's prescription. She saw him at the pharmacy. He told her he'd seen her with me, the *American teacher*, in the square when Benicio was shot."

"Yes…?"

"Then he said he'd seen the boy from the sketch with his grandmother!"

My mouth falls open, and in this momentary vacuum, Moreau says, "Saw him where?"

"It must have been Helena Donders."

"*Where*, Oliver?"

"That's the thing. Right across the street from where he lives, the artist. He said some of the houses were bought up and renovated in the past year. He doesn't know who owns them. He'd noticed the old woman coming and going weeks ago, but it wasn't until last night that he saw the boy in an upstairs window and then saw the woman moving him away."

I'm already out of the chair, shoving shoes on my feet.

Moreau is carrying the phone to the door. "Stay inside with Seraphina, Oliver," Moreau says. "Do not go *anywhere*, for any reason. This is very, very important."

"We'll call you back, Oliver," I yell from across the room, and Moreau shuts down the phone and hands it to me.

I reach for the gun, his gun. There's a moment when we freeze and gaze at one another. We both know he should tell me to hand it over—at the very least, he should say to put it down. We both know how much trouble he'll be in. Not to mention what will happen to me when the truth emerges.

"You're familiar with the model?" he asks.

I nod.

"Don't fire unless I tell you to," he says.

CHAPTER THIRTY-ONE

The man who drew the sketch is Gaston Dubois. Moreau has known him since childhood. We follow him now into his kitchen, where a series of small family sketches, along with watercolors of rolling hills, line the walls. A sliced baguette lies across a cutting board next to a deflated triangle of Brie and, near that, a white bowl of grapes. The lace curtain is closed, but the tiny holes allow Moreau and me a clear view of the house directly across the street. Moreau drags a stool over and puts a compact spotting scope to his eye.

Gaston points to an upstairs window, rimmed in baby-blue shutters. "There," he says, in English, for my benefit. "That is where I saw the boy." I notice, again, the stain beneath his fingernails.

I study the window, *all* the windows, the front door, the cars parked along the curb. Everything about the street is lovely, quintessential Provence, and yet the air is charged with tension, a spookiness I can't identify. If Benicio were here he'd say, "You're *projecting*, Celia."

"He is the boy from the train?" Gaston asks.

Moreau snaps his head around, answers him in French, and Gaston quickly shuts his mouth.

"How did he know?" I ask.

"Town gossip," Moreau says. "Putting two and two together."

I rub my head and neck, pace in place, stretch my thighs by drawing up my ankles behind me, one at a time, until it burns. I tell myself to be patient, to wait for a sign from Moreau.

"How did the boy look?" I finally ask Gaston. "Did he seem all right?"

Gaston glances at the back of Moreau's head, as if for permission to speak. Moreau continues peering through the lens.

"He was," Gaston says, "like a child from his sleep, or perhaps preparing for his bed."

"Do you mean *tired*? Sleepy?"

"Yes. I think so."

"You think so?"

"It is not so close to see perfectly."

"Could you see his *expression*?"

Without turning around Moreau says, "*D'expression.*" Same word, different pronunciation.

Gaston shifts his weight, stalling.

Moreau turns to hear Gaston's answer.

"Sorrow?" Gaston says. "But, as I say, the distance..."

I should *not* have asked.

"I thought, *Maybe it's a different boy*. But the hair, the grand eyes. I had studied his photograph for my drawing—one does not forget so easily. Then I went to look at the photograph again, but it was not in my box. Strange."

I touch Gaston on the shoulder and say, "We took it, my other boy and I," and even in light of everything else, I feel the need of his forgiveness, which he understands and grants with his eyes.

I turn and squint through the lace. The street is empty, static. Even the air looks like it could be a solid block of Lucite.

But then I'm back to the photo, nailing down the details again.

Gaston says yes, he found it as he walked toward the market, a few streets from here.

"Just lying on the ground?"

"Yes, on the ground, looking up at me."

I nod.

After another moment, I ask Moreau if I can look through the scope and he puts it in my hand.

It's midafternoon. The window shade is drawn. Not a speck of light shows around the edges. I give Moreau back the scope.

I ask Gaston, "And this was the only time you saw the boy?"

"I've already asked him these questions," Moreau says.

"Was it the only time?" I repeat.

"Yes."

"Why were you looking there in the first place?"

"It was by chance—I was checking whether the clouds had come back. Then the—" He looks to Moreau and says, *store enrouleur*? Moreau shrugs, then imitates a window blind rolling up. Gaston goes on, "It flew up very quick and there was the boy. Then the grandmother—"

"She is *not* his grandmother," I say, and Moreau gently pats my arm.

"The old woman took him away and closed the blind. This is all."

I take Gaston's hand, hold up his fingers. "What's this stain under your nails?"

"From the vineyard. Grapes."

"I see." Moreau's brother must work in a vineyard…

I drive my own hands, shaky and sweating, through my hair. It's impossible to remain still. Moreau, on the other hand, is like a statue, a bird dog on point.

"Why is the street so...*vacant*?" I ask.

"The houses were falling down," Gaston says. "They were bought to fix and sell...now the work is finished. Some have new owners but I don't know them. Some are still empty—the one next to the one with the boy, on the far side."

Gaston offers us a beer. We decline, but he goes ahead and pours himself a foamy dark ale, picks up a television guide, and flips through it at the round kitchen table, where he sits by himself. The moment has an uncanny similarity to the hours I spent at home surrounded by "the authorities," waiting, waiting. I am desperately sick of wasting time in this way.

"I see movement inside the house, the lower front window near the door," Moreau says without lowering the scope. "A larger figure strolling past. I'm guessing a man."

A side window flanks Gaston's front door and allows a view of the street Moreau doesn't have in the kitchen. I wander in and glance at the house, see nothing in the window Moreau mentioned, but then I peer up the street and see a figure on the corner at the end of the block.

A man, smoking, wearing the same jacket he wore when he pinioned my throat.

I return to the kitchen, but before I can open my mouth, a phone rings. It takes a moment to realize it's Benicio's phone on the counter where I left it. I don't recognize the number. Moreau looks at me, the phone, me. "Answer it," he says. "It's the call."

"No. Isak said they wouldn't forward it. They're using a vocal specialist or something."

"Answer, *now*." Moreau says.

I nearly drop the phone trying to turn it on. "This is Celia."

"Are you ready?" the man says, same accent, same sickening tone.

I glance at Moreau. He nods.

"Yes," I say.

"Oliver will deliver the money to the Zoo Zurich."

"I'm sorry. Did you say the zoo?"

"Yes."

"In Zurich?"

Moreau squints, steps back, crosses his arms.

"I don't have time to repeat myself," the man says. "Two hours, on the wooden bridge near the Schwarzstorch. The landing at the water. I will have a pram with a baby inside. Oliver will bring the money in large bills carried in two diaper bags. Clearly the largest he can find." He laughs.

"All right," I say, even though Oliver is hundreds of kilometers away from Zurich. And as far as we know, *Benny* is *here*, right across the goddamn street. They *know* this. The man on the train, Moreau's brother, *knows* this.

"The pram contains explosives," he says. "If Oliver tries anything at all, or should a sniper take a shot at me, someone will activate the explosives."

I force myself to say, "What about Benny?"

"He will be pushing the pram."

The line deadens.

I'm shaking from head to foot. The boy in the window—who was he? Why is Moreau's brother hovering down the street? "Isak!" I yell. "Are you there?"

"It's all right. I'm here. Please don't be alarmed by this threat."

"Don't be *alarmed*? Where's the goddamn *vocal* specialist?"

"We changed tactics with the voice—"

"And Oliver is *here*. In Saint-Corbenay. They know this. How the fuck do they think he's going to deliver this money in two hours?"

"First of all, Oliver will not be delivering the money, no matter what. Second, I apologize about the vocal specialist. We decided against it. I couldn't warn you or you wouldn't have sounded so frightened by the call. You understand? They want you to be frightened. It makes them feel in control."

"But they *know* we're here! I don't understand what's happening."

"*How* do they know? Why are you so sure of this?"

I have to stop and think. Clearly, they know Benicio is here. But Oliver and me? Moreau's brother knows we're here. But what if he didn't tell anyone?

I glance up at the dark window. Could they have taken Benny back to Zurich during the night? Or was the boy in the window just some other boy? The old woman actually his grandmother?

"I will phone you back in a few moments," Isak says and is gone.

Moreau is pacing, rubbing his temple, the scope abandoned to the table. He stops to light a cigarette. And then he says something to Gaston in French.

Gaston appears nervous.

I back against the window and crane my neck to see a sliver of Moreau's brother still on the corner smoking, just as *his* brother is, a few feet from where I stand. I could reunite them in this moment. And yet—Moreau and Gaston are suddenly yelling at each other. I understand only the tone, the quick angry gestures.

"What is it?" I ask.

Moreau grips Gaston's collar. The man raises his hands in the air, insisting on something, his voice pleading.

Both are so caught up in their arguing that neither stops me as I grab the phone and bolt from the house.

CHAPTER THIRTY-TWO

I'm on the man so quickly he appears not to have seen me until I shove the gun into his spine.

"Why didn't you tell anyone that we were here?" I say.

He slowly raises his hands.

"Why do they think Oliver and I are still in Zurich?"

He doesn't answer.

"I'm not afraid to shoot you," I say. "I don't give a damn *who* you are." I push him toward the house across from Gaston's. Moreau is now running down the street toward us, ducking quietly, as if dodging bullets.

I keep the gun pressed into the man's back, mindful that he could spin and go for the weapon. I feel the heat coming off his neck.

Moreau immediately grabs the man's shoulder, and now the two stand face-to-face.

"I'm so sorry," I say to Moreau. "I know what he means to you. But Benny is my son."

"Let him go, Celia."

The man jerks his face from me to Moreau. His lips part.

"What's your name?" I ask.

Moreau's face shifts as if he's about to answer for him.

"Adam," the man says.

I shove him to the door. "OK, *Adam*. Open the door."

"Celia. You can't do this. Give me the gun."

"Open it," I say.

His brother glances at the lock. "I can't."

"In five seconds I will shoot my way through you *and* the lock."

"Give me the *gun*," Moreau says.

"I don't have a key," his brother says.

"One. Two."

The man raises his hand and knocks.

"What the fuck?" I say.

Moreau slips to the side and pulls a gun from his jacket, a spare that looks meaner than the one in my hand.

"Open the goddamn door," I say.

"I am," the man says.

I hear movement inside but no voices.

He knocks again.

I don't know what else to do but step slightly to the side of the door, opposite Moreau, and wait and see if someone answers.

Then the sound of footsteps inside, clicking, bolts unlocking. The door opens a slim dark crack; I shove Moreau's brother through it.

In an instant, we are all three standing in front of a man in his undershirt and shorts, as if we've barged in on a leisurely afternoon he'd meant to spend with the television. He has a pear-shaped head and the dark, rounded eyes of surprise.

The living room smells of paint and fresh concrete and new furniture. The walls are bright white and completely bare.

Moreau points his gun at the guy in his underwear and yells at him in French, but his eyes repeatedly dart toward me, to the gun at his brother's back. The man of the house looks as if he's about to piss himself. He raises his hands and backs into a rickety wooden chair. His jaw is wider than his forehead, and when he opens his mouth, nothing comes out. His red, bulbous nose looks more like a growth above the large mustache, the kind worn by so many of the farmers in Europe. The fat on his chin and legs trembles.

"Adam," I say. "Take a seat over there next to your friend." He does as he's told. He and Moreau keep eyeing one another.

"Where is Benny?" I say to the man of the house.

He stutters in French. "*Ne parle pas anglais.*"

"Ask him," I order Moreau. "Tell him he has one minute. After that I'm going to shoot."

Moreau starts to protest.

"Ask him!"

Moreau relays the question to the man—at least I assume he does—then they talk for what feels like five minutes. When they're finished, the man lowers his hands, softening his voice.

"What?" I ask. "What's going on?"

I can feel Moreau's stance loosening, the threat of his tone weakening.

"Tell me!"

"I think we made a mistake," Moreau says. "I don't think he's here."

"Don't believe him, Moreau. Who was the boy in the window?"

"His grandnephew. The woman was his sister, the boy her grandson. The boy became ill while visiting. But they're gone now. They left this morning for Lille, where they're from."

I see a twitch in Adam's eye. "What?" I ask him. "What is it?" But he doesn't speak. "What were you doing on this street? Why did you tell me to stay away? Why steal my computer, only to throw it in a field?"

"You found it?" Moreau asks.

"Answer me!"

"I'm not who you think I am," he says, finally.

I laugh. "No. You're not who *you* think you are. And that's beside the point. Answer my questions."

Moreau lowers his gun. "Celia."

"What are you *doing*?" I say.

"Let me take him to the station and question him. We have the wrong house. As far as his...involvement, I can figure that out at the station with my colleagues."

"No. I don't care who he is. He *knows* where Benny is. He *threatened* me. There are laws against that alone. You're not thinking straight."

The man of the house has his face in his hands. Is he weeping?

"What about the photograph Gaston found of Benny just blocks from here?"

"This is a small town, Celia. We know Benny was taken off the train here, and someone here must have been waiting, but—"

I raise my gun to Adam's face and click off the safety. "Indeed, someone was. Why are you here, Adam? Particularly, why *here*, now, on this street?"

"Put the gun down!" Moreau yells. "Or I will take you to the station as well."

Adam glances at Moreau and then me.

"Where the hell is my son?"

Moreau pulls out his cell and prepares to hit speed dial.

"Wait!" I say. "Give me a goddamn *second*."

The man of the house reaches for something on the side table, and I jump, aiming my gun at him. He plucks a tissue from a box and blows his nose.

This ordinary gesture somehow brings everything to a halt. Everyone appears stunned, unable to figure out what our next move should be. If the boy upstairs wasn't Benny, then perhaps all that is left to imagine is that Benny is in Zurich, pushing a pram full of explosives. And whatever Isak has planned, a decoy, perhaps, made to look like Oliver, could easily fail.

"Celia. Look at me," Moreau says. "Do you understand? Gaston was mistaken."

His brother leans forward and studies Moreau. The man in the chair is indeed *weeping*, and as I stare at his shaking shoulders I feel on the verge of tears myself. I slowly lower my gun. But the thought that Benny could have been *right upstairs*, looking out the window, looking for *me*...I can't just let it go. Moreau, on the other hand, is done. He got what he wanted. Benny means nothing to him now.

"But he's my *son*," I say, choking on the words. I suck in my bottom lip to stop the quivering.

"Isak said he would call right back. We have to trust—"

"Suddenly you think trusting Isak is the answer? You're not fooling anyone, Moreau. Is this the kind of reasoning you had when your ex-partner was wounded on the job?"

Moreau's face turns stony. "Shut up," he says.

"Are you going to shoot me?"

Moreau brandishes the cell. "No. But I will arrest you if you don't put the gun on the floor this minute."

The gun dangles in my hand at my side.

"I'm going to take a quick look around upstairs," I say.

Moreau tilts his head and sighs. Moments drag on as if we're engaged in a glaring contest. Finally, Moreau gestures his head toward the stairs. "Go. Two minutes. But leave the gun with me."

I laugh. "Sorry. No."

I turn toward the kitchen, and it is then that the room behind me, and everyone it, radiates the strangest, heaviest silence I've ever felt. Something is *wrong*. It's as if I'm being watched, scrutinized by evil, by someone or something preparing to attack me. But who? I glance back and the weeping man's eyes lock onto mine before he quickly looks away.

Every ounce of sense in me says get the hell out. *Do not wait. Do not look back.* But how do I manage it without going through the living room?

I peek into the kitchen for a back door, and that's when it hits me.

"Hold it," I tell Moreau, and pull up my e-mail on Benicio's phone, point the photo of Benny sent to me by *Mine*, line it up near the corner of the kitchen table, and it's as if the photo were one puzzle piece, and the view of the kitchen from where I stand, the other. They match perfectly. The lampshade, the electric socket on the wall behind.

First I shoot the man of the house. He crashes to the floor as Rémy scrambles out of the way. I fire again, and Rémy never makes it to the door.

CHAPTER THIRTY-THREE

As far as I can tell, Moreau has rushed to help his brother, who is now shrieking and scurrying wildly across the floor.

I've retreated to a corner of the kitchen, briefly worried that Moreau will kill me. There is indeed a back door, but I'll be damned if I'm leaving now. When I hear what sounds like Moreau calling for help on his phone, I bolt to the stairs and take them two at a time. The hallway at the top is so dark I can't believe it's midday. My breathing is loud enough to hear above the howling, above Moreau crying Rémy's name over and over and over.

Every window is covered, every door closed. I grab the first knob, twist it silently, crack the door a couple of inches, and sunlight slashes into the hallway. I thrust the door the rest of the way open and look in, gun raised. Empty, floor to ceiling, bare wires where a light fixture should be.

Sirens have begun in the distance.

I hold still and try to orientate myself to the outside, to the window where Gaston says he saw Benny. It's got to be the door at the end of the hall.

The handle turns an inch. I kneel and try to gauge the sturdiness of the wood and the lock mechanism, then decide there's no time. All I can do is scream out, "Benny!" with all the anguish welled up in me, back against the wall opposite, then rush forward shoulder first, do it again, then again, then turn sideways and start kicking with my heel until at last the jamb splinters and the door whangs open.

The room is so dark I can barely make out a human shape slumped in a folding metal chair directly before me. I snap my gun up. The hem of a dress comes into view, a thick calf, a woman's shoe. Whoever she is, she's not moving.

"Hands on your head," I say, but she doesn't so much as twitch. I grope my free hand along the wall near the door until I feel a switch. When light floods the room, I assume the woman I'm looking at is Helena Donders. She's older, late sixties probably. I don't know if she's dead or just knocked out. I kick her foot and it rolls to the side.

I call out Benny's name again, listen, but all I hear is the rising, staccato pitch of the sirens. I'm in a young child's room, I realize—it's full of babyish toys, stuffed animals. And I realize, too, that it's L-shaped, and that the rest is out of view around a corner. The window blind is crudely sealed to the frame with duct tape. On a child-sized wooden desk beneath it sits Benny's backpack.

One keening siren suddenly stops, two more coming in its wake.

"*Ben-ny*!" I yell again. I slide along the wall, just far enough to sneak a look around the corner. "*Benny*? It's *Mutti*."

A foot. A woman's, cast sideways onto the floor as if she's leaning off the edge of a bed. It stirs.

I step out and point the gun. No, I'm not surprised to see her here. Exactly as I said from the very first day: Isabel. But Benny is draped across her lap, his head tilted back, like some god-awful painting, mother and child, in tragedy, in death.

Isabel doesn't even look up. She rocks him, her sobbing drowned out by the next wave of sirens.

"Get away from him!" I yell.

She won't look at me.

I step forward and place the gun directly on her skull. "Now."

"I'm sorry," she whispers.

I grab a fistful of hair and yank her to the floor. Benny tumbles off the bed with her. She reaches for him and I stick the gun in her face, press hard into her cheek. Our days in Mexico gush back like a putrid taste on my tongue. "Touch him again and you're dead."

A commotion has broken out downstairs. Police? Ambulance? It sounds as if ten people have burst into the front room, shoving furniture across the floor, yelling over one another.

Oh god. I jostle Benny's arm and it flops like a rag doll's. For an instant, I wonder if he's *real.* I grope at his wrist for a pulse but can't locate it. His skin is warm, so I feel my way toward his carotid.

"What did you *do* to him?" I hiss.

Before Isabel can answer, I stroke his cheek, saying, "I'm here, sweetheart. Wake *up. Please.*"

Cops are stampeding up the staircase, pounding across the hardwood floors.

"What's *wrong* with him?" I cry.

Isabel shakes her head at Benny, her tears so pathetic, so reprehensible I leap up and slam the butt of the pistol against her head. It fails to explode into a million glittering shards. She simply falls to the side without a sound. For half a second, I regard her with the detachment of a passing angel…then I reenter my body, and bring the pistol down again in the same spot, raise up and do it again, and again, each time harder, my sickening grunts like the residue of my darkest dream.

PART FOUR

CHAPTER THIRTY-FOUR

Six years ago, after being stationed in Böblingen, Germany, with his first-generation American-born Hungarian wife, Rémy, a US marine, began having visions of a boy he recognized as his brother, though according to his adoption record, he'd been an only child. The visions infiltrated his sleep, came during the days in drowsy unguarded moments: a big man was slinging this *brother* of his across the ground, dragging him, slapping his face. Another boy was present too, and all three tried to free themselves from the man's massive fist. Then, suddenly, the other boys were gone, and the man had Rémy by the back of the neck, lifting his feet off the ground as if he were no weightier than a kitten.

At first, the visions stopped there.

But the longer he lived in Europe, the more memories surfaced: Being taken to a strange, stark house, understanding nothing, not where he was, or where he'd come from, or who was putting him through this, and always, at some point, he would begin to wail through long cold nights. The memories went from unsettling to profoundly disruptive; he had panic attacks, and he had periods of debilitating weakness that rendered him motionless, gasping for breath, sweat soaked, this soldier who'd grown up with loving and gentle parents in a small New Hampshire town, who'd never seen battle.

He was eventually given an honorable discharge but refused to return to the States. For the next few years, he and Mariska were vagabonds, taking short-term jobs in one town after another, alert to the possibility that Rémy would come upon something to tie his visions to the real world. It wasn't until they met a group of Romani one night, in a bar on the outskirts of Dijon, that he got the first glimmer. He'd never known any Romani, but he felt a weird affinity at once, and the more he got into their good graces—helping them diagnose the electrical problem with their ancient truck, offering aspirin to a young woman with cramps, even stitching up the lacerated scalp of one of their elders—the more convinced he was that he had a history with these people, that the village he was searching for was here somewhere in the South of France. He remembered a small white dog named Bisou, a woman calling to it across a yard, *Bisou, Bisou, Bisou. Kiss, kiss, kiss.* The woman calling after the dog was French, he was sure of it—sometimes he heard the same voice speak endearments, to *him. Mon chou, mon coco, bonhomme.* He remembered lavender and thyme on a hillside, the bare rocky jut of a mountain in the distance. He remembered a fountain in the yard, and its concrete seal, spouting water from a broken nose. And then, one day, according to this story, Rémy happened upon Moreau's house. He was struck by the wafting scent of lavender and thyme. He stopped and peered through Moreau's gate and knew.

This is all fine from Moreau's perspective, his way of assuring me that Rémy was a good soul from the start. But it wasn't until Moreau told me how his brother was connected to Benny that I began to feel the full weight of remorse for having shot him in the shoulder, followed by immense gratitude that I'd been such a poor aim.

It's been nine months since the day I found Benny. Nine months since I learned how much Rémy risked to find the truth about himself, and in turn, to try to stop another boy he didn't even know from losing his past too.

Rémy had overheard Pascal, one of the Romani men he'd befriended, talking about being approached by Gunari, a man Pascal had only half-known growing up, offering a lot of money for help with a *poaching* job. Pascal had laughed off the idea, but Rémy went behind his back and offered up his own services. Rémy was, after all, a former marine, with expertise they could use. He spoke French fluently and knew the area well.

Pieter Donders didn't fully trust Rémy at first, and Jonathon didn't trust him at all, especially after he'd lost the photograph of Benny in Saint-Corbenay—the only actual slipup Rémy made, and which caused a brief fistfight between them, Rémy and Pieter Donders. In the end Jonathon *used* Rémy, making him believe he was part of the plan, then flipping that plan on its head, making Rémy the scapegoat. Jonathon even planted the idea in Moreau's ear during his visit: a man he'd heard about from the train, describing Rémy, who had himself been told by Pieter, days before the kidnapping, that the whole thing was called off. Rémy never bought it, and Pieter knew he wouldn't, acting purposely suspicious when he delivered the news. Rémy removed his wedding band before boarding the train in Zurich that day, a small, symbolic gesture to remove Mariska from whatever might happen to him. These people were dangerous. Rémy quickly caught on to Pieter's plan after Benny went missing and the passengers had piled out of the train, when he spotted Helena Watson describing his own clothes and hands to the police. How easy would it have been to pin a kidnapping, or worse, on a man with a mentally unstable past? She gave a detailed and practiced description of Rémy, exactly as her son, Pieter, had instructed. And the photo of Benny that was e-mailed to me? A joke that Pieter thought hilarious.

CHAPTER THIRTY-FIVE

Moreau was prepared to quit the force, but with the return of his brother, he retired with full benefits. It was fitting that Benny should be his last case. Moreau had come full circle, his life's work finally realized. Isak sent him a two-hundred-euro bottle of champagne with a note that read: *Je vous souhaite la paix pour vous et votre famille* (I am wishing peace for you and your family). He and Madame Moreau immediately opened it with Rémy and Mariska, who, for now, have moved into their home.

As for Petit, Moreau finally explained that he'd been a constant companion of Rémy and Moreau's when they were growing up. In fact, Petit was the other boy from Rémy's memories in the vineyard that day. But what Rémy couldn't quite recall or comprehend was the very thing Moreau and Petit could never forget—in the mayhem, Moreau had grabbed hold of Petit, and in doing so, allowed the man to escape with Rémy. Petit never forgave himself, never stopped thinking he should have been the one taken, never stopped feeling indebted to Moreau.

Of course, Moreau's work isn't completely done just yet. He still has to testify at Jonathon's trial. In the meantime, Jonathon no longer looks out onto the sculpture in the courtyard, no longer feels the sun on his face. He was relocated to a maximum-security facility near Berne, where he will spend twenty-three hours a day alone for the rest of his life. If only this were enough to make us feel safe. Enough that we can avoid the new measures he's forced upon us. And Jonathon isn't the only one we worry about. Helena and her sad, wounded boyfriend, along with Pieter, are behind bars awaiting trial, but Gunari is still on the loose, as are several others whom Isak believes played a role in Benny's abduction. Not even he can say for sure how many were involved.

Then there's Isabel.

Turns out, she may be the only weakness Jonathon ever had. The only person, if you can grant him such a capacity, that he ever *loved*. He trusted her. He told everyone, from the start, that they'd never see a dime unless they followed his plan for her explicitly.

And this had been his plan:

Isabel and Benny would wind up in Costa Rica, along with my money. They would blend into a small village and never be seen again. Simple enough. Instead of Benny, the boy who was supposed to push the pram in the Zurich zoo was a Roma boy who looked like him and whom Jonathon intended to sacrifice—the pram was to detonate after Pieter was far enough out of sight with the money, killing both Oliver and the boy instantly.

Isabel was never going to go along with this. By the time she realized what Jonathon's coded letters to her meant, Isak's people had sprung her from jail. She told them everything she knew. They pretended not to believe her. But of course, her visa was immediately approved for Switzerland, after which she easily slipped into France.

Jonathon had meant for me to go on living while both my children were dead—not to mention Benicio. Isak knew all this, which is why he wouldn't tell me *any* of it. His only mistake was losing track of Isabel, unprepared as everyone was, that Benicio would be shot in the middle of the square, throwing the whole town into pandemonium. Still, it is a mistake I can't bear to think about. Benny's whereabouts hadn't yet been revealed to Isabel. No one actually knew where he was, including Isak. If not for Gaston spotting Benny in that one split second—what then? Who would have saved him?

Isabel. After Pieter told her where to find Benny, she had no intention of letting anyone hurt him, no plans to take him away. By the time I arrived, she'd already coldcocked Helena for giving Benny way too much sedative when he wouldn't stop crying. From the beginning, Isabel had put herself in harm's way, knowingly pitting herself against Jonathon to save Benny. She knew what Jonathon was capable of, and, believing no one was on her side, risked her own life for Benny's. It was I who nearly killed her in the end. I don't remember much of what happened after she hit the floor. All I know is what I've been told. If it hadn't been for the police pulling me off of her, she would not have survived.

The truth is, I would have liked to visit her in the hospital before she returned to a life of freedom in Mexico. I would have liked to apologize. But I wasn't allowed anywhere near her. I wasn't allowed anywhere.

CHAPTER THIRTY-SIX

People say one of the hardest things about the death of someone you love is not being able to say good-bye. Perhaps this is true. I wasn't there when the casket was lowered into the ground; I can only imagine the scene. The September air causing mourners to stand their collars on end, the leaves rustling above the bright green lawn. How lovely the white granite tombstone with his name: *Benicio Francisco Martinez. Beloved husband and father.*

One could argue he was never a husband or a father. One could. But no matter. I don't allow myself to grieve for the life we had. It's gone, as surely as yesterday no longer exists. I focus on today. I have to, for Benny.

He sits flush against me in the backseat of the black sedan. I don't know who the driver is. I've never seen him before and we're not allowed to speak. Tinted windows turn the world outside an artificial green, but Benny doesn't mention it. After being found, his first words to me were, "They told me you were dead." He's said very little since.

We've just left a safe house near Marseille, where we've been living a strange, dreamlike existence for nine months. We spent

Christmas alone, a morose affair, the only good to come of which was my attempt at baking Christmas cookies. Benny stepped in to correct the amount and variety of spices I was about to dump into the mixing bowl. It wasn't much, but it was something.

Riding in the car now, I feel the haze of what's happened to us beginning to lift. Benny stretches forward to see out the window, and I kiss the back of his hand cupped tightly inside mine. He's grown slightly taller, his features shifting toward the man he will one day become. He's starting to look more like Isabel.

In just a few moments, we'll be boarding a private plane. All I can think of is how very different this journey is from the one where our story began. I catch Benny studying my face when he thinks I'm not looking. I can only imagine how troubled he must be by my appearance, how tough it must be for him to trust me. I smile down at him and he reciprocates with a mournful smile, the only kind he's shown in the months since he was recovered. It's as if the drugs used to sedate him haven't quite worn off. His psychiatrist says he needs more time. I want to believe this is true. There is so much I want to believe.

* * *

The plane's wheels hit the tarmac and I rifle once more in my bag for our German passports.

"Safe and sound," I whisper, feeling a little drunk, though I haven't had a drop. Even so, elation blossoms beneath my skin.

I still clutch Benny's hand and refuse to let go as we deplane down a set of rickety metal stairs. The blustery wind whips our hair, the sky above clear and baby blue. We're immediately ushered toward the Berlin Brandenburg terminal by two men who pull our luggage along but won't look me in the eye. We enter through a heavy metal door that requires a code, which one of the men swiftly punches into a pad.

They steer us out around the customs lines and in through another coded door, and it isn't until I turn around that I realize the men have disappeared. Benny and I have been deposited in the terminal as if we'd just arrived, like anybody.

Benny looks up at me, terrified.

"It's all right." I hold him against me, momentarily frightened myself. I don't know where we're going. I don't know what's supposed to happen next—Isak was purposely unclear. How close I came to going to prison for attempted murder, how thin the line between one life and its opposite, between losing *everything* you've ever cared about, and getting to keep just enough to carry on. It's appalling, really, if you let yourself think about it.

"This way, love," I say, mustering fake confidence as we head toward the exit, making our way past a long glass partition etched with the word *Willkommen*. And then I see his shoulders through the crowd, recognize his smooth gait. Before I know it he's upon us, straight-faced, seemingly calm. "*Kann ich Ihnen helfen?*" he asks of our bags, and shivers coat me all over like fresh glitter. Benny jerks his head up, recognizing the voice, but then he slips behind me, untrusting, gripping my hand so fiercely it hurts.

"It's OK, *Schatz*," I whisper near his ear. "It's really him."

"*Ja. Bitte*," I say of the bags, smiling at the offer to help. I knew he wouldn't look the same but I didn't know what to expect. The scruffy beard looks remarkable on him. "*Vielen Dank*," I say, wheeling a suitcase toward him. The scars on his temple and forehead have been expertly removed. Barely a trace remains. Perhaps this is just love talking. Whatever it is, I am flush with it. His lighter, shaggier hair and green contacts are equally as attractive to me as his once dark strands and amber eyes used to be.

He briefly touches the back of my hand and I have to turn away to stifle my tears. I caress the back of my short hair, flip the choppy blond strands up and down. I like the way it feels. Fresh. Free. New. My long dark waves are a thing of the past, as are my gray-blue eyes. I'm still shocked by my own reflection, but the new look goes well with my horn-rimmed glasses and brown contacts. I feel updated. A modern version. Celia 2.0. Make that 3.0.

"After you, hot fondue," he whispers, and I have to force a straight face as we stroll toward the exit. "You look sunny," he adds, and I smile, thinking of my mother when I was young, my father calling her "sunny honey." I think of Oliver too, and his endurable, upbeat, steady spirit. He and Pinto are living in Berlin under assumed names—Pinto now goes by Fido, Oliver having picked, he said, the *doggiest* name he could come up with. He's trying his hand at writing for *The Berliner*, while Seraphina, whose aunt passed away just days after we found Benny, finishes classes at the Freie Universität. All of this came secondhand through Isak. I take it on faith that it's the truth.

We can't predict the future, and there's no telling the man Benny will become. All I can do is trust that the light will return fully to his eyes. And already, look at him, hearing Benicio's voice—there's a flicker...

We'll never be able to live a public life again, since we don't, technically, *exist*. I'll never write that book about the missing boy—not that I have the least desire to. But I *will* write again, sooner or later. I'll just have to start over, under a nom de plume, as the French say.

"*Auf diese Weise?*" Benny asks, pointing to the exit.

"*Ja, Schatz*. This way."

See us piling into a taxicab. A family like any other, on our way home.

ACKNOWLEDGMENTS

My deepest and most heartfelt gratitude to you, David Long—teacher, mentor, wordsmith, editor extraordinaire. You have taught me so much about the cabinetry, and worked tirelessly to help make this novel worthy of your treasured and exclusive list of books you've read in 2012.

I want to thank Victoria Griffith, Andrew Bartlett, Alex Carr, Jacque Ben-Zekry, and everyone else at Thomas & Mercer for so much hard work and so many kind efforts on my behalf. You are wildly funny record-holder stellar human beings.

Thank you, Sharon Harrigan, so very much for your constant attention to my work, and to my spirit—and always on such short notice. You're a godsend.

Thank you, Rachel Hoffman and Melissa Crisp, for so graciously combing through the manuscript with me in the eleventh hour and for giving me the courage to let it go.

Thank you, Leigh Camacho Rourks, Rima Karami, Monica Spoelstra Metz, Jessica Donnell, Stephanie Sutherland, Stephanie Howard, Jennifer Greenleaf, Stefin McCargar, Jessica Anya Blau, and Laurie Holst for reading my work, encouraging me, and remaining fast friends.

Thank you, Deanna Dorsey Smith, for getting the state of Wisconsin to buy my books, Shirley Evans for doing the same in Ohio, and Connie Brown for bringing in the Michigan readers.

Thanks, Mom and Dad, for telling everyone you know that I'm a writer, and the rest of my family for cheering me on and spreading the word about my books.

Thank you, Dylan Brown-Reed-Walsdorf (what could I do?), Kelley Burnett, and Liam Reed for being the most awesome and brilliant young people to share a life with.

And, as always, thank you, Andrew Reed, for everything, but this time especially for being so much like Benicio by helping me carry on and laugh in the face of so much madness.

ABOUT THE AUTHOR

Photograph by Andrew Reed, 2011

Audrey Braun is the pen name of novelist Deborah Reed, author of the best seller *Carry Yourself Back to Me*, a Best Book of 2011 Amazon Editors' Pick. As Audrey Braun, she is also the author of the best-selling thriller *A Small Fortune*, the first in a planned trilogy featuring Celia Hagen and her family. After having lived all over the United States and in Europe, Reed currently resides in the Pacific Northwest with her family.